"... *Time grayed to its end. In the four millionth year, he stopped the machine and discovered that there was dry air around him ...*"

He was in the city. But it was not such a city as he had ever seen or imagined, he couldn't follow the wild geometry of the titanic structures that loomed about him and they were never the same. The place throbbed and pulsed with incredible forces, it wavered and blurred in a strangely unreal light. Great devastating energies flashed and roared around him—lightning come to Earth. The air missed and stung with their booming passage.

The thought was a shout filling his skull, blazing along his nerves, too mighty a thought for his stunned brain to do more than grope after meaning:

CREATURE FROM OUT OF TIME, LEAVE THIS PLACE AT ONCE OR THE FORCES WE USE WILL DESTROY YOU!

Through and through him that mental vision seared, down to the very molecules of his brain, his life lay open to Them in a white flame of incandescence.

Can you help me? he cried to the gods. *Can you send me back through time?*

MAN, THERE IS NO WAY TO TRAVEL FAR BACKWARD IN TIME, IT IS INHERENTLY IMPOSSIBLE. YOU MUST GO ON TO THE VERY END OF THE UNIVERSE. AND BEYOND THE END. BECAUSE THAT WAY LIES—

He screamed with the pain of unendurably great thought and concept filling his human brain. . . .

ALIGHT IN THE VOID
by
Poul Anderson

Also by Poul Anderson
Published by Tor Books

The Boat of a Million Years
Hoka! (with Gordon R. Dickson)
The Longest Voyage
A Midsummer Tempest
No Truce with Kings
The Saturn Game
The Shield of Time
Tales of the Flying Mountains
Tales of the Time Patrol [forthcoming]

POUL ANDERSON
ALIGHT
IN THE VOID

A TOM DOHERTY ASSOCIATES BOOK
NEW YORK

ALIGHT IN THE VOID

Copyright © 1991 by Poul Anderson

A Tor Book
Published by Tom Doherty Associates, Inc.
49 West 24th Street
New York, N.Y. 10010

Cover art by Paul Chadwick

ISBN: 0-812-50874-2

First edition: April 1991

Printed in the United States of America

0 9 8 7 6 5 4 3 2 1

ACKNOWLEDGMENTS

"Terminal Quest," "Earthman, Beware!," "The Star Beast," and "Flight to Forever" all appeared originally in *Super Science Stories*, and are copyright by Fictioneers, Inc., respectively © 1951, © 1951, © 1950, and © 1950. "Son of the Sword" originally appeared in *Adventure Magazine*, and is copyright © 1951 by Popular Publications, Inc. "Ballade of an Artificial Satellite" originally appeared in *The Magazine of Fantasy and Science Fiction*, and is copyright © 1958 by Mercury Press, Inc.

CONTENTS

INTRODUCTION:
"Tell Me a Story"

"Tell me a story."

We ask for it over and over in our childhoods, and listen enchanted. Scarcely any of us ever outgrows the wish. Those few who have done so are as pitiable as those who believe they have no further need of love. Stories are a part of being human. I have little doubt that Neanderthal men and women sat around the campfire hearing of ancestors and animals, hunters and heroes, gods and ghosts. Quite likely, in a more primitive fashion, *Homo erectus* did. Certainly narratives are among the oldest writings that have come down to us. Epics helped weld tribes into nations, while folk tales not only amused, but conveyed much unpretentious wisdom and heartened people for a life that was largely hard.

Children make up little fantasies of their own,

to color the times when their elders aren't taking them into wonderland. Most of them forget how as they become adults, and simply pass on what has happened to them in real life or what they have from others. A lucky few keep the ability, develop it, become the daydreamers on behalf of everybody else. Once they were bards, sagamen, shanachies, whatever form their art took in their particular societies. Writers were accessible only to the few who had access to books and could read, except when one of those read aloud to an audience. Printing and widespread literacy changed that. Eventually almost anyone could satisfy the desire for a story, directly and inexpensively.

In the course of the nineteenth century, publishers came to realize that many people had distinct preferences in fiction. Some wanted adventure, some wanted romance, some wanted cowboys or crime or—the list was long. This doesn't mean these people were all dolts who wouldn't read anything outside a narrow field. Most were not. However, they liked to know what they were getting. After all, the majority were workers, students, and others who couldn't afford to buy blindly.

The publishers obliged by issuing periodicals devoted to specialized fiction. These became known as pulp magazines, because they were printed on cheap, un-glossy paper, generally with untrimmed edges. The idea was to keep costs down so that the product, which drew negligible advertising revenue, could sell for a dime or, at most, a quarter. Another economy measure was to pay the writers as little as possible, often not until publication and then perhaps only on threat of lawsuit. I must add that this was not universal practice. Some houses with more working capital offered a better deal. Indeed, the dividing line between the pulps and the high-circulation, high-paying "slicks" was a vague one. Though the latter did not overtly categorize their fiction, their editorial policies were frequently so rigid that there was more artistic freedom in the former.

The pulp vices were crudity and carelessness, predictable when a writer had to get manuscripts out fast if he wanted to pay the rent. "Crudity" does not mean coarseness; language was decorous, and insofar as sex came in at all, it was in the form of a chaste love interest. "Carelessness" does not mean indifference; writers might put on a show of being cynical hacks, but in fact nearly all of them did the best job that circumstances and their own abilities permitted. Many cared desperately for what they were doing, as did many of the illustrators. The two words mean simply that time was seldom available to search for the absolutely right phrase or to consider characters and their backgrounds in exquisite detail.

This was less harmful than it may seem. The better professionals were skilled craftsmen, who told good, well-constructed stories in good, well-constructed prose. A number moonlighted at it, and those among them who chose to were thus able to produce work as lapidary as anything in the slicks or even the "literary" magazines, and usually more original. Also, when high polish was not required, beginners had a chance, earning while they learned. A number who later became world-famous got their start in humble magazines devoted to mysteries, Westerns, adventure, science fiction, and fantasy. There, too, well-known writers would find a home for something that had not fitted into the limited slick market.

The pulps mostly bore names like *Thrilling Western Stories*, *Black Mask Detective Stories*, or *Astounding Stories of Super-Science*. Their covers were apt to be just as gaudy, commonly featuring a macho man defending a terrified maiden from some villainy or other. The blurbs—editorial descriptions of what a story was supposedly about—matched this, and so did the titles that editors might foist on tales. Hence "pulp" became synonymous with "sensationalism" and "trash" in the minds of those who didn't buy it.

While the publishers brought this on themselves to a considerable extent, it wasn't fair. Some pulps were pretty dreadful, but most provided honest popular entertainment; and the best—notably in the mystery and science fiction fields—did pioneering undreamed-of in the offices of *The Saturday Evening Post* or *Collier's* or, for that matter, *The Atlantic Monthly*.

For the pulp virtues were as real as the pulp vices, and rather more important. They included color, narrative pace, basic human emotion, and occasional innovative ideas or writing styles. These stories were not for the ages, alongside the works of Dickens, Twain, or Kipling. Only a few are still remembered, though those bid fair to go on in print for a long time yet. But they were no stagnant backwater of literature, either. They were a perhaps small but definitely vital part of its mainstream—the real mainstream, not the academic pigeonhole—and they helped set the direction it has taken since.

Today the pulp magazines are gone, except for a handful of modestly earning, relatively respectable successors. Now and then somebody makes a valiant attempt to found another one, but nearly always fails. Likewise for the literary magazines; and what slicks we have are far from what slicks used to be. Probably television had the most to do with bringing on the mass extinction. It may well also be killing creative imagination in our children.

Times change, you can't go home again, and pulp-type fiction does flourish more lustily than ever before, in the paperback original book. Yet we have lost something—the glamour of distant lands that few had ever beheld, a steam locomotive whistling lonesome at midnight, the smell of rough-textured paper between garish covers . . . innocence.

Herewith a sample of my own contributions to the era as it neared its end. Afterward I learned how to write better, but the visions are no more clear, the dreams no more bright—and maybe less so, now—than they were when all the world was young.

—Poul Anderson
Orinda, California

TERMINAL QUEST

THE SUN WOKE HIM.

He stirred uneasily, feeling the long shafts of light slant over the land. The muted gossip of birds became a rush of noise and a small wind blew till the leaves chattered at him. Wake up, wake up, wake up, Rugo, a new day is on the hills and you can't lie sleeping, wake up!

The light reached under his eyelids, roiling the darkness of dreams. He mumbled and curled into a tighter knot, drawing sleep back around him like a cloak, sinking toward the dark and the unknowningness with his mother's face before him.

She laughed down the long ways of night, calling and calling, and he tried to follow her, but the sun wouldn't let him.

Mother, he whimpered. *Mother, please come back, mother.*

1

She had gone and left him, once very long ago. He had been little then and the cave had been big and gloomy and cold, and there were flutterings and watchings in the shadows of it and he had been frightened. She had said she was going after food, and had kissed him and gone off down the steep moonlit valley. And there she must have met the Strangers, because she never came back. And he had cried for a long time and called her name, but she didn't return.

That had been so long ago that he couldn't number the years. But now that he was getting old, she must have remembered him and been sorry she left, for lately she often came back at night.

The dew was cold on his skin. He felt the stiffness in him, the ache of muscle and bone and dulling nerve, and forced himself to move. If he stirred all at once, stretching himself and not letting his throat rasp with the pain of it, he could work the damp and the cold and the earth out, he could open his eyes and look at the new day.

It was going to be hot. Rugo's vision wasn't so good anymore, the sun was only a blur of fire low on the shadowy horizon, and the mist that streamed through the dales turned it ruddy. But he knew that before midday it would be hot.

He got up, slowly climbing to all four feet, pulling himself erect with the help of a low branch. Hunger was a dull ache in him. He looked emptily around at the thicket, a copse of scrub halfway up the hillside. There were the bushes and the trees, a hard summer green that would be like metal later in the day. There were

2

the dead leaves rustling soggily underfoot, still wet with the dew that steamed away in white vapors. There were birds piping up the sun, but nowhere food, nowhere anything to eat.

Mother, you said you would bring back something to eat.

He shook his big scaly head, clearing out the fog of dreams. Today he would have to go down into the valley. He had eaten the last berries on the hillside, he had waited here for days with weakness creeping from his belly through his bones, and now he would have to go down to the Strangers.

He went slowly out of the thicket and started down the hillside. The grass rustled under his feet, the earth quivered a little beneath his great weight. The hill slanted up to the sky and down to the misty dales, and he was alone with the morning.

Only grass and the small flowers grew here. Once the hills had been tall with forest; he recalled cool shadowy depths and the windy roar of the treetops, small suns spattered on the ground and the drunken sweetness of resin smell in summer and the blaze of broken light from a million winter crystals. But the Strangers had cut down the woods and now there were only rotting stumps and his blurred remembering. His alone, for the men who had hewed down the forest were dead and their sons never knew—and when he was gone, who would care? Who would be left to care?

He came to a brook that rushed down the hillside, rising from a spring higher up and flowing to join the Thunder River. The water was cold and clean and he drank heavily, slopping it into him with both hands and wriggling his tail with the refreshment of it. This much remained to him, at least, though the source was dwindling now that the watershed was gone. But he would be dead before the brook was dry, so it didn't matter too much.

He waded over it. The cold water set his lame foot to tingling and needling. Beyond it he found the old logging trail and went down that. He walked slowly, not being eager to do what he must, and tried to make a plan.

The Strangers had given him food now and then, out of charity or in return for work. Once he had labored almost a year for a man, who had given him a place to sleep and as much as he wanted to eat—a good man to work for, not full of the hurry which seemed to be in his race, with a quiet voice and gentle eyes. But then the man had taken a woman, and she was afraid of Rugo, so he had had to leave.

A couple of times, too, men from Earth itself had come to talk to him. They had asked him many questions about his people. How had they lived, what was their word for this and that, did he remember any of their dances or music? But he couldn't tell them much, for his folk had been hunted before he was born, he had seen a flying-thing spear his father with flame and later his mother had gone to look for food and not come back. The men from Earth had, in fact, told him more than he could give them, told him about cities and books and gods which his people had had, and if he had wanted to learn these things from the Strangers they could have told him more. They, too, had paid him something, and he had eaten well for a while.

I am old now, thought Rugo, *and not very strong. I never was strong, beside the powers they have. One of us could drive fifty of them before him—but one of them, seated at the wheel of a thing of metal and fire, could reap a thousand of us. And I frighten their women and children and animals. So it will be hard to find work, and I may have to beg a little bread for no more return than going away. And the grain that they will feed me grew in the soil of this world; it is strong with the bones of my father and fat with the flesh of my mother. But one must eat.*

When he came down into the valley, the mists had lifted in ragged streamers and already he could feel the heat of the sun. The trail led onto a road, and he turned north toward the human settlements. Nobody was in sight yet, and it was quiet. His footfalls rang loud on the pavement, it was hard under his soles and the impact of walking jarred up into his legs like small sharp needles. He looked around him, trying to ignore the hurting.

They had cut down the trees and harrowed the land and sowed grain of Earth, until now the valley lay open to the sky. The brassy sun of summer and the mordant winds of winter rode over the deep glens he remembered, and the only trees were in neat orchards bearing alien fruit. It was as if these Strangers were afraid of the dark, as if they were so frightened by shadows and half-lights and rustling unseen

5

distances that they had to clear it all away, one sweep of fire and thunder and then the bright inflexible steel of their world rising above the dusty plains.

Only fear could make beings so vicious, even as fear had driven Rugo's folk to rush, huge and scaled and black, out of the mountains, to smash houses and burn grain fields and wreck machines, even as fear had brought an answer from the Strangers which heaped stinking bodies in the ruins of the cities he had never seen. Only the Strangers were more powerful, and their fears had won.

He heard the machine coming behind him, roaring and pounding down the road with a whistle of cloven air flapping in its wake, and remembered in a sudden gulping that it was forbidden to walk in the middle of the road. He scrambled to one side, but it was the wrong one, the side they drove on, and the truck screamed around him on smoking tires and ground to a halt on the shoulder.

A Stranger climbed out, and he was almost dancing with fury. His curses poured forth so fast that Rugo couldn't follow them. He caught a few words: "Damned weird thing. . . . Coulda killed me. . . . Oughta be shot. . . . Have the law on yuh. . . ."

Rugo stood watching. He had twice the height of the skinny pink shape that jittered and railed before him, and some four times the bulk, and though he was old, one sweep of his hand would stave in the skull and spatter the brains on the hot hard concrete. Only all the power of the Strangers was behind the creature, fire and ruin

6

and flying steel, and he was the last of his folk and sometimes his mother came at night to see him. So he stood quietly, hoping the man would get tired and go away.

A booted foot slammed against his shin, and he cried out with the pain of it and lifted one arm the way he had done as a child when the bombs were falling and metal rained around him.

The man sprang back. "Don't yuh try it," he said quickly. "Don't do nothing. They'll hunt yuh down if yuh touch me."

"Go," said Rugo, twisting his tongue and throat to the foreign syllables which he knew better than the dimly recalled language of his people. "Please go."

"Yuh're on'y here while yuh behave yuhrself. Keep yuhr place, see. Nasty devil! Watch yuhrself." The man got back into the truck and started it. The spinning tires threw gravel back at Rugo.

He stood watching the machine, his hands hanging empty at his sides, until it was beyond his aging sight. Then he started walking again, careful to stay on the correct edge of the road.

Presently a farm appeared over a ridge. It lay a little way in from the highway, a neat white house sitting primly among trees with its big outbuildings clustered behind it and the broad yellowing grainfields beyond. The sun was well into the sky now, mist and dew had burned away, the wind had fallen asleep. It was still and hot. Rugo's feet throbbed with the hardness of the road.

He stood at the entrance, wondering if he

should go in or not. This was a rich place, they'd have machines and no use for his labor. When he passed by here before, the man had told him shortly to be on his way. But they could perhaps spare a piece of bread and a jug of water, just to be rid of him or maybe to keep him alive. He knew he was one of the neighborhood sights, the last native. Visitors often climbed up his hill to see him and toss a few coins at his feet and take pictures while he gathered them.

He puzzled out the name on the mailbox. *Elias Whately.* He'd try his luck with Elias Whately.

As he came up the driveway a dog bounded forth and started barking, high shrill notes that hurt his ears. The animal danced around and snapped with a rage that was half panic. None of the beasts from Earth could stand the sight and smell of him; they knew he was not of their world and a primitive terror rose in them. He remembered the pain when teeth nipped his rheumatic legs. Once he had killed a dog that bit him, a single unthinking swipe of his tail, and the owner had fired a shotgun at him. His scales had turned most of the charge, but some was still lodged deep in his flesh and bit him again when the days were cold.

"Please," he said to the dog. His bass rumbled in the warm still air and the barking grew more frantic. "Please, I will not harm, please do not bite."

"*O-oh!*"

The woman in the front yard let out a little scream and ran before him, up the steps and through the door to slam it in his face. Rugo sighed, feeling suddenly tired. She was afraid.

8

They were all afraid. They had called his folk trolls, which were something evil in their old myths. He remembered that his grandfather, before he died in a shelterless winter, had called them torrogs, which he said were pale bony things that ate the dead, and Rugo smiled with a wryness that was sour in his mouth.

But little use in trying here. He turned to go.

"You!"

He turned back to face the tall man who stood in the door. The man held a rifle, and his long face was clamped tight. Behind him peeked a red-headed boy, maybe thirteen years old, a cub with the same narrow eyes as his father.

"What's the idea of coming in here?" asked the man. His voice was like the grating of iron.

"Please, sir," said Rugo, "I am hungry. I thought if I could do some work, or if you had any scraps—"

"So now it's begging, eh?" demanded Whately. "Don't you know that's against the law? You could be put in jail. By heaven, you ought to be! Public nuisance, that's all you are."

"I only wanted work," said Rugo.

"So you come in and frighten my wife? You know there's nothing here for a savage to do. Can you run a tractor? Can you repair a generator? Can you even eat without slobbering it on the ground?" Whately spat. "You're a squatter on somebody else's land, and you know it. If I owned that property you'd be out on your worthless butt so fast you wouldn't know which end was up.

"Be glad you're alive! When I think of what you murdering slimy monsters did— Forty

9

years! Forty years, crammed in stinking space-ships, cutting themselves off from Earth and all the human race, dying without seeing ground, fighting every foot of all the light-years, to get to Tau Ceti—and then you said the Earthmen couldn't stay! Then you came and burned their homes and butchered women and children! The planet's well rid of you, all the scum of you, and it's a wonder somebody doesn't take a gun and clear off the last of the garbage." He half lifted his weapon.

It was no use explaining, thought Rugo. Maybe there really had been a misunderstanding, as his grandfather had claimed, maybe the old counselors had thought the first explorers were only asking if more like them could come and had not expected settlers when they gave permission—or maybe, realizing that the Strangers would be too strong, they had decided to break their word and fight to hold their planet.

But what now? The Strangers had won the war, with guns and bombs and a plague virus that went like a scythe through the natives; they had hunted the few immunes down like animals, and now he was the last of his kind in all the world and it was too late to explain.

"Sic 'im, Shep!" cried the boy. "Sic 'im! Go get 'im!"

The dog barked in closer, rushing and retreating, trying to work its cowardice into rage.

"Shut up, Sam," said Whately to his son. Then to Rugo, "Get!"

"I will leave," said Rugo. He tried to stop the trembling that shuddered in him, the nerve-

10

wrenching fear of what the gun could spit. He was not afraid to die, he thought sickly, he would welcome the darkness when it came— but his life was so deep-seated, he would live and live and live while the slugs tore into him. He might take hours to die.

"I will be on my way, sir," he said.

"No, you won't," snapped Whately. "I won't have you going down to the village and scaring little kids there. Back where you came from!"

"But, sir—please—"

"Get!" The gun pointed at him, he looked down the muzzle and turned and went out the gate. Whately waved him to the left, back down the road.

The dog charged in and sank its teeth in an ankle where the scales had fallen away. He screamed with the pain of it and began to run, slowly and heavily, weaving in his course. The boy Sam laughed and followed him.

"Nyaah, nyaah, nyaah, ugly ol' troll, crawl back down in yuhr dirty ol' hole!"

After a while there were other children, come from the neighboring farms in that timeless blur of running and raw lungs and thudding heart and howling, thundering noise. They followed him, and their dogs barked, and the flung stones rattled off his sides with little swords where they struck.

"Nyaah, nyaah, nyaah, ugly ol' troll, crawl back down in yurh dirty ol' hole!"

"Please," he whispered. "Please."

When he came to the old trail he hardly saw it. The road danced in a blinding flimmer of heat

11

and dust, the world was tipping and whirling about him, and the clamor in his ears drowned out their shrilling. They danced around him, sure of their immunity, sure of the pain and the weakness and the loneliness that whimpered in his throat, and the dogs yammered and rushed in and nipped his tail and his swollen legs.

Presently he couldn't go on. The hillside was too steep, there was no will left to drive his muscles. He sat down, pulling in knees and tail, hiding his head in his arms, hardly aware in the hot, roaring, whirling blindness that they stoned him and pummeled him and screamed at him.

Night and rain and the west wind crying in high trees, a cool wet softness of grass and the wavering little fire, the grave eyes of my father and the dear lost face of my mother— Out of the night and the rainy wind and the forest they hewed down, out of the years and the blurring memories and the shadowland of dreams, come to me, mother, come to me and take me in your arms and carry me home.

After a while they grew tired of it and went away, some turning back and some wandering higher up into the hills after berries. Rugo sat unmoving, buried in himself, letting a measure of strength and the awareness of his pain seep back.

He burned and pulsed, jagged bolts shot through his nerves, his throat was too dry for swallowing and the hunger was like a wild animal deep in his belly. And overhead the sun swam in a haze of heat, pouring it down over him, filling the air with an incandescence of arid light.

After still a longer time, he opened his eyes. The lids felt raw and sandy, vision wavered as if the heat-shimmer had entered his brain. A man stood watching him.

Rugo shrank back, lifting a hand before his face. But the man stood quietly, puffing away on a battered old pipe. He was shabbily dressed and carried a rolled bundle on his shoulders.

"Had a pretty rough session there, didn't you, old-timer?" he asked. His voice was soft. "Here." He bent a lanky frame over the crouching native. "Here, you need a drink."

Rugo lifted the canteen to his lips and gulped till it was empty. The man looked him over. "You're not too banged up," he decided. "Just cuts and abrasions; you trolls always were a tough breed. I'll give you some aneurine, though."

He fished a tube of yellow salve out of one pocket and smeared it on the wounds. The hurt eased, faded to a warm tingle, and Rugo sighed.

"You are very kind, sir," he said unsurely.

"Nah. I wanted to see you anyway. How you feel now? Better?"

Rugo nodded slowly, trying to stop the shivers which still ran in him. "I am well, sir," he said.

"Don't 'sir' me. Too many people'd laugh themselves sick to hear it. What was your trouble, anyway?"

"I—I wanted food, sir—pardon me. I w-wanted food. But they—he—told me to go back. Then the dogs came, and the young ones—"

"Kids can be pretty gruesome little monsters at times, all right. Can you walk, old fella? I'd like to find some shade."

Rugo pulled himself to his feet. It was easier than he had thought it would be. "Please, if you will be so kind, I know a place with trees—"

The man swore, softly and imaginatively. "So that's what they've done. Not content with blotting out a whole race, they have to take the guts from the last one left. Look, you, I'm Manuel Jones, and you'll speak to me as one free bum to another or not at all. Now let's find your trees."

They went up the trail without speaking much, though the man whistled a dirty song to himself, and crossed the brook and came to the thicket. When Rugo lay down in the light-speckled shade it was as if he had been born again. He sighed and let his body relax, flowing into the ground, drawing of its old strength.

The human started a fire and opened some cans in his pack and threw their contents into a small kettle. Rugo watched hungrily, hoping he would give him a little, ashamed and angry with himself for the way his stomach rumbled. Manuel Jones squatted under a tree, shoved his hat off his forehead and got his pipe going afresh.

Blue eyes in a weatherbeaten face watched Rugo with steadiness and no hate nor fear. "I've been looking forward to seeing you," he said. "I wanted to meet the last member of a race which could build the Temple of Otheii."

"What is that?" asked Rugo.

"You don't *know*?"

14

"No, sir—I mean, pardon me, no, Mr. Jones—"

"Manuel. And don't you forget it."

"No, I was born while the Strangers were hunting the last of us—Manuel. We were always fleeing. I was only a few years old when my mother was killed. I met the last other Gunnur—member of my race—when I was only about twenty. That was almost two hundred years ago. Since then I have been the last."

"God," whispered Manuel. "God, what a race of free-wheeling devils we are!"

"You were stronger," said Rugo. "And anyway it is very long ago now. Those who did it are dead. Some humans have been good to me. One of them saved my life; he got the others to let me live. And some of the rest have been kind."

"Funny sort of kindness, I'd say." Manuel shrugged. "But as you put it, Rugo, it's too late now."

He drew heavily on his pipe. "Still, you had a great civilization. It wasn't technically minded like ours, it wasn't human or fully understandable to humans, but it had its own greatness. Oh, it was a bloody crime to slaughter you, and we'll have to answer for it some day."

"I am old," said Rugo. "I am too old to hate."

"But not too old to be lonesome, eh?" Manuel's smile was lopsided. He fell into silence, puffing blue clouds into the blaze of air.

Presently he went on, thoughtfully, "Of course, one can understand the humans. They were the poor and the disinherited of our land-hungry Earth, they came forty years over empty space with all their hopes, giving their lives to the ships so their children might land—and then your council forbade it. They *couldn't* return, and man never was too nice about his methods when need drove him. They were lonely and scared, and your hulking horrible appearance made it worse. So they fought. But they needn't have been so thorough about it. That was sheer hellishness."

"It does not matter," said Rugo. "It was long ago."

They sat for a while in silence, huddled under the shade against the white flame of sunlight, until the food was ready.

"Ah." Manuel reached gratefully for his eating utensils. "It's not too good, beans and stuff, and I haven't an extra plate. Mind just reaching into the kettle?"

"I—I— It is not needful," mumbled Rugo, suddenly shy again.

"The devil it isn't! Help yourself, old-timer, plenty for all."

The smell of food filled Rugo's nostrils, he could feel his mouth going wet and his stomach screaming at him. And the Stranger really seemed to mean it. Slowly, he dipped his hands into the vessel and brought them out full and ate with the ungraceful manners of his people.

Afterward they lay back, stretching and sighing and letting the faint breeze blow over them. There hadn't been much for one of Rugo's size, but he had emptied the kettle and was more full than he had been for longer than he could well recall.

"I am afraid this meal used all your supplies," he said clumsily.

"No matter," yawned Manuel. "I was damn sick of beans anyway. Meant to lift a chicken tonight."

"You are not from these parts," said Rugo. There was a thawing within him. Here was someone who seemed to expect nothing more than friendship. You could lie in the shade beside him and watch a lone shred of cloud drift over the hot blue sky and let every nerve and muscle go easy. You felt the fullness of your stomach, and you lolled on the grass, and idle words went from one to another, and that was all there was and it was enough.

"You are not a plain tramp," he added thoughtfully.

"Maybe not," said Manuel. "I taught school a good many years ago, in Cetusport. Got into a bit of trouble and had to hit the road and liked it well enough not to settle down anywhere else. Hobo, hunter, traveler to any place that sounds interesting—it's a big world and there's enough in it for a lifetime. I want to get to know this New Terra planet, Rugo. Not that I mean to write a book or any such nonsense. I just want to know it."

He sat up on one elbow. "That's why I came to see you," he said. "You're part of the old world, the last part of it except for empty ruins and a few torn pages in museums. But I have a notion that your race will always haunt us, that no matter how long man is here something of you will enter into him." There was a half mystical look on his lean face. He was not the dusty

17

tramp now but something else which Rugo could not recognize.

"The planet was yours before we came," he said, "and it shaped you and you shaped it; and now the landscape which was yours will become part of us, and it'll change us in its own slow and subtle ways. I think that whenever a man camps out alone on New Terra, in the big hills where you hear the night talking up in the trees, I think he'll always remember something. There'll always be a shadow just beyond his fire, a voice in the wind and in the rivers, something in the soil that will enter the bread he eats and the water he drinks, and that will be the lost race which was yours."

"It may be so," said Rugo unsurely. "But we are all gone now. Nothing of ours is left."

"Some day," said Manuel, "the last man is going to face your loneliness. We won't last forever either. Sooner or later age or enemies or our own stupidity or the darkening of the universe will come for us. I hope that the last man can endure life as bravely as you did."

"I was not brave," said Rugo. "I was often afraid. They hurt me, sometimes, and I ran."

"Brave in the way that counts," said Manuel.

They talked for a while longer, and then the human rose. "I've got to go, Rugo," he said. "If I'm going to stay here for a while, I'll have to go down to the village and get a job of some sort. May I come up again tomorrow and see you?"

Rugo got up with him and wrapped the dignity of a host about his nakedness. "I would be honored," he said gravely.

He stood watching the man go until he was lost to sight down the curve of the trail. Then he sighed a little. Manuel was good, yes, he was the first one in a hundred years who had not hated or feared him, or been overly polite and apologetic, but had simply traded words as one free being to another.

What had he said? "One free bum to another." Yes, Manuel was a good bum.

He would bring food tomorrow, Rugo knew, and this time there would be more said, the comradeship would be wholly easy and the eyes wholly frank. It pained him that he could offer nothing in return.

But wait, maybe he could. The farther hills were thick with berries, some must still be there even this late in the season. Birds and animals and humans couldn't have taken them all, and he knew how to look. Yes, he could bring back a great many berries, that would go well with a meal.

It was a long trip, and his sinews protested at the thought. He grunted and set out, slowly. The sun was wheeling horizonward, but it would be a few hours yet till dark.

He went over the crest of the hill and down the other side. It was hot and quiet, the air shimmered around him, leaves hung limp on the few remaining trees. The summer-dried grass rustled harshly under his feet, rocks rolled aside and skittered down the long slope with a faint click. Beyond, the range stretched into a blue haze of distance. It was lonely up here, but he was used to that and liked it.

Berries—yes, a lot of them clustered around

Thunder Falls, where there was always coolness and damp. To be sure, the other pickers knew that as well as he, but they didn't know all the little spots, the slanting rocks and the wet crannies and the sheltering overgrowths of brush. He could bring home enough for a good meal.

He wound down the hillside and up the next. More trees grew here. He was glad of the shade and moved a little faster. Maybe he should pull out of this district altogether. Maybe he would do better in a less thickly settled region, where there might be more people like Manuel. He needed humans, he was too old now to live off the country, but they might be easier to get along with on the frontier.

They weren't such a bad race, the Strangers. They had made war with all the fury that was in them, had wiped out a threat with unnecessary savagery; they still fought and cheated and oppressed each other; they were silly and cruel and they cut down the forests and dug up the earth and turned the rivers dry. But among them were a few like Manuel, and he wondered if his own people had boasted more of that sort than the Strangers did.

Presently he came out on the slope of the highest hill in the region and started climbing it toward Thunder Falls. He could hear the distant roaring of a cataract, half lost in the pounding of his own blood as he fought his aging body slowly up the rocky slant, and in the dance of sunlight he stopped to breathe and tell himself that not far ahead were shadow and mist and a coolness of rushing waters. And when he was ready to come back, the night would be there to walk home with him.

The shouting falls drowned out the voices of the children, nor had he looked for them since he knew they were forbidden to visit this danger spot without adults along. When he topped the stony ridge and stood looking down into the gorge, he saw them just below and his heart stumbled in sickness.

The whole troop was there, with red-haired Sam Whately leading them in a berry hunt up and down the cragged rocks and along the pebbled beach. Rugo stood on the bluff above them, peering down through the fine cold spray and trying to tell his panting body to turn and run before they saw him. Then it was too late; they had spotted his dark form and were crowding closer, scrambling up the bluff with a wicked rain of laughter.

"Looka that!" He heard Sam's voice faintly through the roar and crash of the falls. "Looky who's here! Ol' Blackie!"

A stone cracked against his ribs. He half turned to go, knowing dully that he could not outrun them. Then he remembered that he had come to gather berries for Manuel Jones, who had called him brave, and a thought came.

He called out in a bass that trembled through the rocks, "Do not do that!"

"Yaah, listen when he says, ha-ha-ha!"

"Leave me alone," cried Rugo, "or I will tell your parents that you were here."

They stopped then, almost up to him, and for a moment only the yapping dogs spoke. Then

Sam sneered at him. "Aw, who'd lissen to yuh, ol' troll?"

"I think they will believe me," said Rugo. "But if you do not believe it, try and find out."

They hovered for a moment, unsure, staring at each other. Then Sam said, "Okay, ol' tattle-tale, okay. But you let us be, see?"

"I will do that," said Rugo, and the hard-held breath puffed out of him in a great sigh. He realized how painfully his heart had been fluttering, and weakness was watery in his legs.

They went sullenly back to their berry gathering, and Rugo scrambled down the bluff and took the opposite direction.

They called off the dogs too, and soon he was out of sight of them.

The gorge walls rose high and steep on either side of the falls. Here the river ran fast, green and boiling white, cold and loud as it sprang over the edge in a veil of rainbowed mist. Its noise filled the air, rang between the crags and hooted in the water-hollowed caves. The vibrations of the toppling stream shivered unceasingly through the ground. It was cool and wet here, and there was always a wind blowing down the length of the ravine. The fall wasn't high, only about twenty feet, but the river thundered down it with brawling violence and below the cataract it was deep and fast and full of rocks and whirlpools.

Plants were scattered between the stones, small bushes and a few slender trees. Rugo found some big tsugi leaves and twisted them together into a good-sized bag as his mother had taught him, and started hunting. The berries grew on low, round-leafed bushes that clustered under rocks and taller plants, wherever they could find shelter, and it was something of an art to locate them easily. Rugo had had many decades of practice.

It was peaceful work. He felt his heart and lungs slowing; content and restfulness stole over him. So had he gone with his mother, often and often in the time that was clearer to him than all the blurred years between, and it was as if she walked beside him now and showed him where to look and smiled when he turned over a bush and found the little blue spheres. He was gathering food for his friend, and that was good.

After some time, he grew aware that a couple of the children had left the main group and were following him, a small boy and girl tagging at a discreet distance and saying nothing. He turned and stared at them, wondering if they meant to attack him after all, and they looked shyly away.

"You sure find a lot of them, Mister Troll," said the boy at last, timidly.

"They grow here," grunted Rugo with unease.

"I'm sorry they were so mean to you," said the girl. "Me and Tommy wasn't there or we wouldn't of let them."

Rugo couldn't remember if they had been with the pack that morning or not. It didn't matter. They were only being friendly in the hope he would show them where to find the berries.

Still, no few of the Stranger cubs had liked

23

him in the past, those who were too old to be frightened into screaming fits by his appearance and too young to be drilled into prejudice, and he had been fond of them in turn. And whatever the reason of these two, they were speaking nicely.

"My dad said the other day he thought he could get you to do some work for him," said the boy. "He'd pay you good."

"Who is your father?" asked Rugo uncertainly.

"He's Mr. Jim Stackman."

Yes, Stackman had never been anything but pleasant, in the somewhat strained and awkward manner of humans. They felt guilty for what their grandparents had done, as if that could change matters. But it was something. Most humans were pretty decent; their main fault was the way they stood by when others of their race did evil, stood by and said nothing and felt embarrassed.

"Mr. Whately won't let me go down there," said Rugo.

"Oh, him!" said the boy with elaborate scorn. "My dad'll take care of old Sourpuss Whately."

"I don't like Sam Whately neither," said the girl. "He's mean, like his old man."

"Why do you do as he says, then?" asked Rugo.

The boy looked uncomfortable. "He's bigger'n the rest of us," he muttered.

Yes, that was the way of humans, and it wasn't really their fault that the Manuel Joneses were so few among them. They suffered more for it than anyone else, probably.

"Here is a nice berry bush," said Rugo. "You can pick it if you want to."

He sat down on a mossy bank, watching them eat, thinking that maybe things had changed today. Maybe he wouldn't need to move away after all.

The girl came and sat down beside him. "Can you tell me a story, Mister Troll?" she asked.

"H'm?" Rugo was startled out of his revery.

"My daddy says an old-timer like you must know lots of things," she said.

Why, yes, thought Rugo, he did know a good deal, but it wasn't the sort of tale you could give children. They didn't know hunger and loneliness and shuddering winter cold, weakness and pain and the slow grinding out of hope, and he didn't want them ever to know it. But, well, he could remember a few things besides. His father had told him stories of what had once been, and—

Your race will always haunt us, no matter how long man is here something of you will enter into him.... There'll always be a shadow just beyond the fire, a voice in the wind and in the rivers, something in the soil that will enter the bread he eats and the water he drinks, and that will be the lost race which was yours.

"Why, yes," he said slowly. "I think so."

The boy came and sat beside the girl, and they watched him with large eyes. He leaned back against the bank and fumbled around in his mind.

"A long time ago," he said, "before people had come to New Terra, there were trolls like me

25

living here. We built houses and farms, and we had our songs and our stories just like you do. So I can tell you a little bit about that, and maybe some day when you are grown up and have children of your own you can tell them."

"Sure," said the boy.

"Well," said Rugo, "there was once a troll king named Utorri who lived in the Western Dales, not far from the sea. He lived in a big castle with towers, reaching up so they nearly scraped the stars, and the wind was always blowing around the towers and ringing the bells. Even when the trolls were asleep they could hear the shivering of the bells. And it was a rich castle, whose doors always stood open to any wayfarers, and each night there was a feast where all the great trolls met and music sounded and the heroes told of their wanderings—"

"Hey, look!"

The children's heads turned, and Rugo's annoyed glance followed theirs. The sun was low now, its rays were long and slanting and touched the hair of Sam Whately with fire where he stood. He had climbed up on the highest crag above the falls and balanced swaying on the narrow perch, laughing. The laughter drifted down through the boom of waters, faint and clear in the evening.

"Gee, he shouldn't," said the little girl.

"I'm the king of the mountain!"

"Young fool," grumbled Rugo.

"I'm the king of the mountain!"

"Sam, come down—" The child's voice was almost lost in thunder.

26

He laughed again and crouched, feeling with his hands along the rough stone for a way back. Rugo stiffened, remembering how slippery the rocks were and how the river hungered.

The boy started down, and lost his hold and toppled.

Rugo had a glimpse of the red head as it rose over the foaming green. Then it was gone, snuffed like a torch as the river sucked it under.

Rugo started to his feet, yelling, remembering that even now he had the strength of many humans and that a man had called him brave. Some dim corner of his mind told him to wait, to stop and think, and he ran to the shore with the frantic knowledge that if he did consider the matter wisely he would never go in.

The water was cold around him, it sank fangs of cold into his body and he cried out with the pain.

Sam's head appeared briefly at the foot of the cataract, whirling downstream. Rugo's feet lost bottom and he struck out, feeling the current grab him and yank him from shore.

Swimming, whipping downstream, he shook the water from his eyes and gasped and looked wildly around. Yes, there came Sam, a little above him, swimming with mindless reflex.

The slight body crashed against his shoulder. Almost, the river had its way, then he got a clutch on the arm and his legs and tail and free hand were working.

They whirled on down the stream and he was deaf and blind and the strength was spilling from him like blood from an open wound.

There was a rock ahead. Dimly he saw it

through the cruel blaze of sunlight, a broad flat stone rearing above a foam of water. He flailed, striving for it, sobbing the wind into his empty lungs, and they hit with a shock that exploded in his bones.

Wildly he grabbed at the smooth surface, groping for a handhold. One arm lifted Sam Whately's feebly stirring body out, fairly tossed it on top of the rock, and then the river had him again.

The boy hadn't breathed too much water, thought Rugo in his darkening brain. He could lie there till a flying-thing from the village picked him up. *Only—why did I save him? Why did I save him? He stoned me, and now I'll never be able to give Manuel those berries. I'll never finish the story of King Utorri and his heroes.*

The water was cool and green around him as he sank. He wondered if his mother would come for him.

A few miles farther down, the river flows broad and quiet between gentle banks. Trees grow there, and the last sunlight streams through their leaves to glisten on the surface. This is down in the valley, where the homes of man are built.

Earthman, Beware!

As he neared the cabin, he grew aware that someone was waiting for him.

He paused for a moment, scowling, and sent his perceptions ahead to analyze that flash of knowledge. Something in his brain thrilled to the presence of metal, and he caught subtler overtones of the organic—oil and rubber and plastic . . . He dismissed it as an ordinary small helicopter and concentrated on the faint, maddeningly elusive fragments of thought, nervous energy, lifeflows between cells and molecules. There was only one person, and the sketchy outline of his data fitted only a single possibility.

Margaret.

For another instant he stood quietly. His primary emotion was sadness. He felt annoyance, perhaps a subtle dismay that his hiding place had finally been located, but mostly it was pity that held him. Poor Peggy. Poor kid.

Well—he'd have to have it out. He straightened his slim shoulders and resumed his walk.

The Alaskan forest was quiet around him. A faint evening breeze rustled the dark pines and drifted past his cheeks, a cool lonesome presence in the stillness. Somewhere birds were twittering as they settled toward rest, and the mosquitoes raised a high, thin buzz as they whirled outside the charmed circle of odorless repellent he had devised. Otherwise, he heard only the scrunch of his footsteps on the ancient floor of needles. After two years of silence, the vibrations of human presence were like a great shout along his nerves.

When he came out into the little meadow, the sun was going down behind the northern hills. Long aureate rays slanted across the grass, touching the huddled shack with a wizard glow and sending enormous shadows before them. The helicopter was a metallic dazzle against the darkling forest, and he was quite close before his blinded eyes could discern the woman.

She stood in front of the door, waiting, and the sunset turned her hair to ruddy gold. She wore the red sweater and the navy-blue skirt she had worn when they had last been together, and her slim hands were crossed before her. So she had waited for him many times when he came out of the laboratory, quiet as an obedient child. She had never turned her pert vivacity on him, not after noticing how it streamed off his uncomprehending mind like rain off one of the big pines.

He smiled lopsidedly. "Hullo, Peggy," he said, feeling the blind inadequacy of words. But what could he say to her?

"Joel . . ." she whispered.

He saw her start and felt the shock along her nerves. His smile grew more crooked, and he nodded. "Yeah," he said. "I've been bald as an egg all my life. Out here, alone, I had no reason to use a wig."

Her wide hazel eyes searched him. He wore backwoodsman's clothes, plaid shirt and stained jeans and heavy shoes, and he carried a fishing rod and tackle box and a string of perch. But he had not changed, at all. The small slender body, the fine-boned ageless features, the luminous dark eyes under the high forehead, they were all the same. Time had laid no finger on him.

Even the baldness seemed a completion, letting the strong classic arch of his skull stand forth, stripping away another of the layers of ordinariness with which he had covered himself.

He saw that she had grown thin, and it was suddenly too great an effort to smile. "How did you find me, Peggy?" he asked quietly.

From her first word, his mind leaped ahead to the answer, but he let her say it out. "After you'd been gone six months with no word, we—all your friends, insofar as you ever had any—grew worried. We thought maybe something had happened to you in the interior of China. So we started investigating, with the help of the Chinese government, and soon learned you'd never gone there at all. It had just been a red herring, that story about investigating Chinese archaeological sites, a blind to gain time while you—disappeared. I just kept on hunting, even after everyone else had given up, and finally Alaska occurred to me. In Nome I picked up rumors of an odd and unfriendly squatter out in the bush. So I came here."

"Couldn't you just have let me stay vanished?" he asked wearily.

"No." Her voice was trembling with her lips. "Not till I knew for sure, Joel. Not till I knew you were safe and—and—"

He kissed her, tasting salt on her mouth, catching the faint fragrance of her hair. The broken waves of her thoughts and emotions washed over him, swirling through his brain in a tide of loneliness and desolation.

Suddenly he knew exactly what was going to happen, what he would have to tell her and the responses she would make—almost to the word, he foresaw it, and the futility of it was like a leaden weight on his mind. But he had to go through with it, every wrenching syllable must come out. Humans were that way, groping through a darkness of solitude, calling to each other across abysses and never, never understanding.

"It was sweet of you," he said awkwardly. "You shouldn't have, Peggy, but it was . . ." His voice trailed off and his pre-vision failed. There were no words which were not banal and meaningless.

"I couldn't help it," she whispered. "You know I love you."

"Look, Peggy," he said "This can't go on. We'll have to have it out now. If I tell you who I am, and why I ran away—" He tried to force cheerfulness. "But never have an emotional scene on an empty stomach. Come on in and I'll fry up these fish."

"I will," she said with something of her old spirit. "I'm a better cook than you."

It would hurt her, but: "I'm afraid you couldn't use my equipment, Peggy."

He signaled to the door, and it opened for him. As she preceded him inside, he saw that her face and hands were red with mosquito bites. She must have been waiting a long time for him to come home.

"Too bad you came today," he said desperately. "I'm usually working in here. I just happened to take today off."

She didn't answer. Her eyes were traveling around the cabin, trying to find the immense order that she knew must underlie its chaos of material.

He had put logs and shingles on the outside to disguise it as an ordinary shack. Within, it might have been his Cambridge laboratory, and she recognized some of the equipment. He had filled a plane with it before leaving. Other things she did not remember, the work of his hands through two lonely years, jungles of wiring and tubing and meters and less understandable apparatus. Only a little of it had the crude, unfinished look of experimental setups. He had been working on some enormous project of his own, and it must be near its end now.

But after that—?

The gray cat which had been his only real companion, even back in Cambridge, rubbed against her legs with a mew that might be recognition. *A friendlier welcome than* he *gave me*, she thought bitterly, and then, seeing his grave eyes on her, flushed. It was unjust. She had hunted him out of his self-chosen solitude, and he had been more than decent about it.

Decent—but not human. No unattached human male could have been chased across the world by an attractive woman without feeling more than the quiet regret and pity he showed.

Or did he feel something else? She would never know. No one would ever know all which went on within that beautiful skull. The rest of humanity had too little in common with Joel Weatherfield.

"The *rest* of humanity?" he asked softly.

She started. That old mind-reading trick of his had been enough to alienate most people. You never knew when he would spring it on you, how much of it was guesswork based on a transcendent logic and how much was—was . . .

He nodded. "I'm partly telepathic," he said, "and I can fill in the gaps for myself—like Poe's Dupin, only better and easier. There are other things involved too—but never mind that for now. Later."

He threw the fish into a cabinet and adjusted several dials on its face. "Supper coming up," he said.

"So now you've invented the robot chef," she said.

"Saves me work."

"You could make another million dollars or so if you marketed it."

"Why? I have more money right now than any reasonable being needs."

"You'd save people a lot of time, you know."
He shrugged.

She looked into a smaller room where he must live. It was sparsely furnished, a cot and a desk and some shelves holding his enormous microprinted library. In one corner stood the multitone instrument with which he composed the music that no one had ever liked or understood. But he had always found the music of man shallow and pointless. And the art of man and the literature of man and all the works and lives of man.

"How's Langtree coming with his new encephalograph?" he asked, though he could guess the answer. "You were going to assist him on it, I recall."

"I don't know." She wondered if her voice reflected her own weariness. "I've been spending all my time looking, Joel."

He grimaced with pain and turned to the automatic cook. A door opened in it and it slid out a tray with two dishes. He put them on a table and gestured to chairs. "Fall to, Peggy."

In spite of herself, the machine fascinated her. "You must have an induction unit to cook that fast," she murmured, "and I suppose your potatoes and greens are stored right inside it. But the mechanical parts—" She shook her head in baffled wonderment, knowing that a blueprint would have revealed some utterly simple arrangement involving only ingenuity.

Dewed cans of beer came out of another cabinet. He grinned and lifted his. "Man's greatest achievement. Skoal."

She hadn't realized she was so hungry. He ate more slowly, watching her, thinking of the incongruity of Dr. Margaret Logan of MIT wolfing fish and beer in a backwoods Alaskan cabin.

Maybe he should have gone to Mars or some outer-planet satellite. But no, that would have involved leaving a much clearer trail for anyone to follow—you couldn't take off in a spaceship as casually as you could dash over to China. If he had to be found out, he would rather that she did it. For later on she'd keep his secret with the stubborn loyalty he had come to know.

She had always been good to have around, ever since he met her when he was helping MIT on their latest cybernetics work. Twenty-four-year-old Ph.D.'s with brilliant records were rare enough—when they were also good-looking young women, they became unique. Langtree had been quite hopelessly in love with her, of course. But she had taken on a double program of work, helping Weatherfield at his private laboratories in addition to her usual duties—and she planned to end the latter when her contract expired. She'd been more than useful to him, and he had not been blind to her looks, but it was the same admiration that he had for landscapes and thoroughbred cats and open space. And she had been one of the few humans with whom he could talk at all.

Had been. He exhausted her possibilities in a year, as he drained most people in a month. He had known how she would react to any situation, what she would say to any remark of his, he knew her feelings with a sensitive perception beyond her own knowledge. And the loneliness had returned.

But he hadn't anticipated her finding him, he

thought wryly. After planning his flight he had not cared—or dared—to follow out all its logical consequences. Well, he was certainly paying for it now, and so was she.

He had cleared the table and put out coffee and cigarettes before they began to talk. Darkness veiled the windows, but his fluorotubes came on automatically. She heard the far faint baying of a wolf out in the night, and thought that the forest was less alien to her than this room of machines and the man who sat looking at her with that too brilliant gaze.

He had settled himself in an easy chair and the gray cat had jumped up into his lap and lay purring as his thin fingers stroked its fur. She came over and sat on the stool at his feet, laying one hand on his knee. It was useless to suppress impulses when he knew them before she did.

Joel sighed. "Peggy," he said slowly, "you're making a hell of a mistake."

She thought, briefly, how banal his words were, and then remembered that he had always been awkward in speech. It was as if he didn't feel the ordinary human nuances and had to find his way through society by mechanical robot.

He nodded. "That's right," he said.

"But what's the matter with you?" she protested desperately. "I know they all used to call you 'cold fish' and 'brain-heavy' and 'animated vacuum tube,' but it isn't so. I know you feel more than any of us do, only—only—"

"Only not the same way," he finished gently.

"Oh, you always were a strange sort," she

37

said dully. "The boy wonder, weren't you? Obscure farm kid who entered Harvard at thirteen and graduated with every honor they could give at fifteen. Inventor of the ion-jet space drive, the controlled-disintegration ion process, the cure for the common cold, the crystalline-structure determination of geological age, and only Heaven and the patent office know how much else. Nobel prize winner in physics for your relativistic wave mechanics. Pioneer in a whole new branch of mathematical series theory. Brilliant writer on archaeology, economics, ecology, and semantics. Founder of whole new schools in painting and poetry. What's your IQ, Joel?"

"How should I know? Above 200 or so, IQ in the ordinary sense becomes meaningless. I was pretty foolish, Peggy. Most of my published work was done at an early age, out of a childish desire for praise and recognition. Afterward, I couldn't just stop—conditions wouldn't allow it. And of course I had to do something with my time."

"Then at thirty, you pack up and disappear. *Why?*"

"I'd hoped they'd think I was dead," he murmured. "I had a beautiful faked crash in the Gobi, but I guess nobody ever found it. Because poor loyal fools like you just didn't believe I could die. It never occurred to you to look for my remains." His hand passed lightly over her hair, and she sighed and rested her head against his knee. "I should have foreseen that."

"Why in hell I should have fallen in love with a goof like you, I'll never know," she said at last. "Most women ran in fright. Even your

38

money couldn't get them close." She answered her own question with the precision of long thought. "But it was sheer quality, I suppose. After you, everyone else became so trite and insipid." She raised her eyes to him, and there was sudden terrified understanding in them. "And is that why you never married?" she whispered.

He nodded compassionately. Then, slowly, he added, "Also, I'm not too interested in sex yet. I'm still in early adolescence, you know."

"No, I don't know." She didn't move, but he felt her stiffen against him.

"I'm not human," said Joel Weatherfield quietly.

"A mutant? No, you couldn't be." He could feel the tensing of her, the sudden rush of wild thought and wordless nerve current, pulse of blood as the endocrines sought balance on a high taut level of danger. It was the old instinctive dread of the dark and the unknown and the hungry presences beyond a dim circle of firelight—she held herself moveless, but she was an animal bristling in panic.

Calmness came, after a while during which he simply sat stroking her hair. She looked up at him again, forcing herself to meet his eyes.

He smiled as well as he could and said, "No, no, Peggy, all this could never happen in one mutation. I was found in a field of grain one summer morning thirty years ago. A . . . woman . . . who must have been my mother, was lying beside me. They told me later she was of my physical type, and that and the curious iridescent garments she wore made them think she was some circus freak. But she was dead, burned and torn by energies against which she had shielded me with her body. There were only a few crystalline fragments lying around. The people disposed of that and buried her.

"The Weatherfields were an elderly local couple, childless and kindly. I was only a baby, naturally, and they took me in. I grew quite slowly physically, but of course mentally it was another story. They came to be very proud of me in spite of my odd appearance. I soon devised the perfect toupee to cover my hairlessness, and with that and ordinary clothes I've always been able to pass for human. But you may remember I've never let any human see me without shirt and pants on.

"Naturally, I quickly decided where the truth must lie. Somewhere there must be a race, humanoid but well ahead of man in evolution, which can travel between the stars. Somehow my mother and I had been cast away on this desert planet, and in the vastness of the universe any searchers that there may be have never found us."

He fell back into silence. Presently Margaret whispered, "How—human—are you, Joel?"

"Not very," he said with a flash of the old candid smile she remembered. How often had she seen him look up from some piece of work which was going particularly well and give her just that look! "Here, I'll show you."

He whistled, and the cat jumped from his lap. Another whistle, and the animal was across the room pawing at a switch. Several large plates were released, which the cat carried back in his mouth.

Margaret drew a shaky breath. "I never yet heard of anyone training a cat to run errands."

"This is a rather special cat," he replied absently, and leaned forward to show her the plates. "These are X-rays of myself. You know my technique of photographing different layers of tissue? I developed that just to study myself. I also confess to exhuming my mother's bones, but they proved to be simply a female version of my own. However, a variation of the crystalline structure method did show that she was at least five hundred years old."

"Five hundred years!"

He nodded. "That's one of several reasons why I'm sure I'm a very young member of my race. Incidentally, her bones showed no sign of age; she corresponded about to a human twenty-five. I don't know whether the natural life span of the race is that great or whether they have artificial means of arresting senility, but I do know that I can expect at least half a millennium of life on Earth. And Earth seems to have a higher gravity than our home world, it's not a very healthy spot for me."

She was too dazed to do more than nod. His finger traced over the X-ray plates. "The skeletal differences aren't too great, but look here and here—the foot, the spine—the skull bones are especially peculiar— Then the internal organs. You can see for yourself that no human being ever had—"

"A double heart?" she asked dully.

"Sort of. It is a single organ, but with more functions than the human heart. Never mind that, it's the neural structure that's most important. Here are several of the brain, taken at different depths and angles."

She fought down a gasp. Her work on encephalography had required a good knowledge of the brain's anatomy. *No human being carries this in his head.*

It wasn't too much bigger than the human. Better organization, she thought; Joel's people would never go insane. There were analogues, a highly convoluted cortex, a medulla, the rest of it. But there were other sections and growths which had no correspondents in any human.

"What are *they*?" she asked.

"I'm not very sure," he replied slowly, a little distastefully. "This one here is what I might call the telepathy center. It's sensitive to neural currents in other organisms. By comparing human reactions and words with the emanations I can detect, I've picked up a very limited degree of telepathy. I can emit, too, but since no human can detect it I've had little use for that power. Then this seems to be for voluntary control of ordinarily involuntary functions—pain blocks, endocrine regulation, and so on—but I've never learned to use it very effectively and I don't dare experiment much on myself. There are other centers—most of them, I don't even know what they're for."

His smile was weary. "You've heard of feral children—the occasional human children who're raised by animals? They never learn to speak, or to exercise any of their specifically human abilities, till they're captured and taught by men. In fact, they're hardly human at all.

"I'm a feral child, Peggy."

She began to cry, deep racking sobs that

42

shook her like a giant's hand. He held her until
it passed and she sat again at his knee with the
slow tears going down her cheeks. Her voice
was a shuddering whisper:

"Oh, my dear, my dear, how lonely you must
have been . . ."

Lonely? No human being would ever know
how lonely.

It hadn't been too bad at first. As a child, he
had been too preoccupied and delighted with
his expanding intellectual horizons to care that
the other children bored him—and they, in their
turn, heartily disliked Joel for his strangeness
and the aloofness they called "snooty." His fos-
ter parents had soon learned that normal standards just didn't apply to him; they kept him
out of school and bought him the books and
equipment he wanted. They'd been able to afford that; at the age of six he had patented, in
old Weatherfield's name, improvements on farm
machinery that made the family more than well-
to-do. He'd always been a "good boy," as far as
he was able. They'd had no cause to regret
adopting him, but it had been pathetically like
the hen who has hatched ducklings and watches
them swim away from her.

The years at Harvard had been sheer heaven,
an orgy of learning, of conversations and
friendship with the great who came to see an
equal in the solemn child. He had had no normal social life then either, but he hadn't missed
it; the undergraduates were dull and a little
frightening. He'd soon learned how to avoid most
publicity—after all, infant geniuses weren't alto-

gether unknown. His only real trouble had been with a psychiatrist who wanted him to be more "normal." He grinned as he remembered the rather fiendish ways in which he had frightened the man into leaving him entirely alone.

But toward the end, he had found limitations in the life. It seemed utterly pointless to sit through lectures on the obvious and to turn in assignments of problems which had been done a thousand times before. And he was beginning to find the professors a little tedious, more and more he was able to anticipate their answers to his questions and remarks, and those answers were becoming ever more trite.

He had long been aware of what his true nature must be though he had had the sense not to pass the information on. Now the dream began to grow in him: To find his people!

What was the use of everything he did, when their children must be playing with the same forces as toys, when his greatest discoveries would be as old in their culture as fire in man's? What pride did he have in his achievements, when none of the witless animals who saw them could say "Well done!" as it should be said? What comradeship could he ever know with blind and stupid creatures who soon became as predictable as his machines: *With whom could he think?*

He flung himself savagely into work, with the simple goal of making money. It hadn't been hard. In five years he was a multimillionaire, with agents to relieve him of all the worry and responsibility, with freedom to do as he chose. To work for escape.

How weary, flat, stale and unprofitable
Seem to me all the uses of this world!

But not of every world! Somewhere, somewhere out among the grand host of the stars. . . .

The long night wore on.

"Why did you come here?" asked Margaret.
Her voice was quiet now, muted with hopelessness.

"I wanted secrecy. And human society was
getting to be more than I could stand."

She winced, then: "Have you found a way to
build a faster-than-light spaceship?"

"No. Nothing I've ever discovered indicates any
way of getting around Einstein's limitation. There
must be a way, but I just can't find it. Not too
surprising, really. Our feral child would probably never be able to duplicate ocean-going ships."

"But how do you ever hope to get out of the
Solar System, then?"

"I thought of a robot-manned spaceship going
from star to star, with myself in suspended an-
imation." He spoke of it as casually as a man
might describe some scheme of repairing a
leaky faucet. "But it was utterly impractical.
My people can't live anywhere near, or we'd
have had more indication of them than one
shipwreck. They may not live in this galaxy at
all. I'll save that idea for a last resort."

"But you and your mother must have been in
some kind of ship. Wasn't anything ever
found?"

"Just those few glassy fragments I mentioned. It makes me wonder if my people use
spaceships at all. Maybe they have some sort of

matter transmitter. No, my main hope is some kind of distress signal which will attract help."

"But if they live so many light-years away—"

"I've discovered a strange sort of—well, you might call it radiation, though it has no relation to the electromagnetic spectrum. Energy fields vibrating a certain way produce detectable effects in a similar setup well removed from the first. It's roughly analogous to the old spark-gap radio transmitters. The important thing is that these effects are transmitted with no measurable time lag or diminution with distance."

She would have been aflame with wonder in earlier times. Now she simply nodded. "I see. It's a sort of ultrawave. But if there are no time or distance effects, how can it be traced? It'd be completely nondirectional, unless you could beam it."

"I can't—yet. But I've recorded a pattern of pulses which are to correspond to the arrangement of stars in this part of the galaxy. Each pulse stands for a star, its intensity for the absolute brightness, and its time separation from the other pulses for the distance from the other stars."

"But that's a one-dimensional representation, and space is three-dimensional."

"I know. It's not as simple as I said. The problem of such representation was an interesting problem in applied topology—took me a good week to solve. You might be interested in the mathematics, I've got my notes here somewhere— But anyway, my people, when they direct those pulses, should easily be able to deduce what I'm trying to say. I've put Sol at the head of each series of pulses, so they'll even know what particular star it is that I'm at. Anyway, there can only be one or a few configurations exactly like this in the universe, so I've given them a fix. I've set up an apparatus to broadcast my call automatically. Now I can only wait."

"How long have you waited?"

He scowled. "A good year now—and no sign. I'm getting worried. Maybe I should try something else."

"Maybe they don't use your ultrawave at all. It might be obsolete in their culture."

He nodded. "It could well be. But what else is there?"

She was silent.

Presently Joel stirred and sighed. "That's the story, Peggy."

She nodded, mutely.

"Don't feel sorry for me," he said. "I'm doing all right. My research here is interesting, I like the country, I'm happier than I've been for a long time."

"That's not saying much, I'm afraid," she answered.

"No, but— Look, Peggy, you know what I am now. A monster. More alien to you than an ape. It shouldn't be hard to forget me."

"Harder than you think, Joel. I love you. I'll always love you."

"But—Peggy, it's ridiculous. Just suppose that I did come live with you. There could never be children . . . but I suppose that doesn't matter too much. We'd have nothing in common, though. Not a thing. We couldn't talk, we couldn't share any of the million little things that make a marriage, we could hardly ever

47

work together. I can't live in human society anymore, you'd soon lose all your friends, you'd become as lonely as I. And in the end you'd grow old, your powers would fade and die, and I'd still be approaching my maturity. Peggy, neither of us could stand it."

"I know."

"Langtree is a fine man. It'd be easy to love him. You've no right to withhold a heredity as magnificent as yours from your race."

"You may be right."

He put a hand under her chin and tilted her face up to his. "I have some powers over the mind," he said slowly. "With your co-operation, I could adjust your feelings about this."

She tensed back from him, her eyes wide and frightened. "No—"

"Don't be a fool. It would only be doing now what time will do anyway." His smile was tired, crooked. "I'm really a remarkably easy person to forget, Peggy."

His will was too strong. It radiated from him, in the lambent eyes and the delicately carved features that were almost human, it pulsed in great drowsy waves from his telepathic brain and seemed almost to flow through the thin hands. Useless to resist, futile to deny—give up, give up and sleep. She was so tired.

She nodded, finally. Joel smiled the old smile she knew so well. He began to talk.

She never remembered the rest of the night, save as a blur of half awareness, a soft voice that whispered in her head, a face dimly seen through wavering mists. Once, she recalled, there was a machine that clicked and hummed, and little lights flashing and spinning in darkness. Her memory was stirred, roiled like a quiet pool; things she had forgotten through most of her life floated to the surface. It seemed as if her mother was beside her.

In the vague foggy dawn, he let her go. There was a deep unhuman calm in her; she looked at him with something of a sleepwalker's empty stare and her voice was flat. It would pass, she would soon become normal again, but Joel Weatherfield would be a memory with little emotional color, a ghost somewhere in the back of her mind.

A ghost. He felt utterly tired, drained of strength and will. He didn't belong here, he was a shadow that should have been flitting between the stars, the sunlight of Earth erased him.

"Good-bye, Peggy," he said. "Keep my secret. Don't let anyone know where I am. And good luck go with you all your days."

"Joel—" She paused on the doorstep, a puzzled frown crossing her features. "Joel, if you can think at me that way, can't your people do the same?"

"Of course. What of it?" For the first time, he didn't know what was coming, he had changed her too much for prediction.

"Just that—why should they bother with gadgets like your ultrawave for talking to each other? They should be able to think between the stars."

He blinked. It had occurred to him, but he had not thought much beyond it, he had been too preoccupied with his work.

"Good-bye, Joel." She turned and walked away through the dripping gray fog. An early sunbeam struck through a chance rift and glanced off her hair. He stood in the doorway until she was gone.

He slept through most of the day. Awakening, he began to think over what had been said.

By all that was holy, Peggy was right! He had immersed himself too deeply in the purely technical problems of the ultrawave, and since then in mathematical research which passed the time of waiting, to stand off and consider the basic logic of the situation. But this—it made sense.

He had only the vaguest notion of the inherent powers of his own mind. Physical science had offered too easy an outlet for him. Nor could he, unaided, hope to get far in such studies. A human feral child might have the heredity of a mathematical genius, but unless he was found and taught by his own kind he would never comprehend the elements of arithmetic—or of speech or sociability or any of the activities which set man off from the other animals. There was just too long a heritage of prehuman and early human development for one man, alone, to recapitulate in a lifetime, when his environment held no indication of the particular road his ancestors had taken.

But those idle nerves and brain centers must be for something. He suspected that they were means of direct control over the most basic forces in the universe. Telepathy, telekinesis, precognition—what godlike heritage had been denied him?

At any rate, it did seem that his race had gone

beyond the need of physical mechanisms. With complete understanding of the structure of the space-time-energy continuum, with control by direct will of its underlying processes, they would project themselves or their thoughts from star to star, create what they needed by sheer thought—and pay no attention to the gibberings of lesser races.

Fantastic, dizzying prospect! He stood breathless before the great shining vision that opened to his eyes.

He shook himself back to reality. The immediate problem was getting in touch with his race. That meant a study of the telepathic energies he had hitherto almost ignored.

He plunged into a fever of work. Time became meaningless, a succession of days and nights, waning light and drifting snow and the slow return of spring. He had never had much except his work to live for, now it devoured the last of his thoughts. Even during the periods of rest and exercise he forced himself to take, his mind was still at the problem, gnawing at it like a dog with a bone. And slowly, slowly, knowledge grew.

Telepathy was not directly related to the brain pulses measured by encephalography. Those were feeble, short-range by-products of neuronic activity. Telepathy, properly controlled, leaped over an intervening space with an arrogant ignoring of time. It was, he decided, another part of what he had labeled the ultrawave spectrum, which was related to gravitation as an effect of the geometry of space-time. But, while gravitational effects were produced by the presence of matter, ultrawave effects came into being when certain energy fields vibrated. However, they did not appear unless there was a properly tuned receiver somewhere. They seemed somehow "aware" of a listener even before they came into existence. That suggested fascinating speculations about the nature of time, but he turned away from it. His people would know more about it than he could ever find out alone.

But the concept of waves was hardly applicable to something that traveled with an "infinite velocity"—a poor term semantically, but convenient. He could assign an ultrawave a frequency, that of the generating energy fields, but then the wavelength would be infinite. Better to think of it in terms of tensors, and drop all pictorial analogies.

His nervous system did not itself contain the ultra-energies. Those were omnipresent, inherent in the very structure of the cosmos. But his telepathy centers, properly trained, were somehow coupled to that great underlying flow, they could impose the desired vibrations on it. Similarly, he supposed, his other centers could control those forces to create or destroy or move matter, to cross space, to scan the past and future probability-worlds, to . . .

He couldn't do it himself. He just couldn't find out enough in even his lifetime. Were he literally immortal, he might still never learn what he had to know; his mind had been trained into human thought patterns, and this was something that lay beyond man's power of comprehension.

But all I need is to send one clear call . . .

He struggled with it. Through the endless winter nights he sat in the cabin and fought to master his brain. How did you send a shout to the stars?

Tell me, feral child, how do you solve a partial differential equation?

Perhaps some of the answer lay in his own mind. The brain has two types of memory, the "permanent" and the "circulating," and apparently the former kind is never lost. It recedes into the subconscious, but it is still there, and it can be brought out again. As a child, a baby, he would have observed things, remembered sights of apparatus and feelings of vibration, which his more mature mind could now analyze.

He practiced autohypnosis, using a machine he devised to help him, and the memories came back, memories of warmth and light and great pulsing forces. Yes—yes, there was an engine of some sort, he could see it thrumming and flickering before him. It took a while before he could translate the infant's alien impressions into his present sensory evaluations, but when that job was done he had a clear picture of—something.

That helped, just a little. It suggested certain types of hookup, empirical patterns which had not occurred to him before. And now slowly, slowly, he began to make progress.

An ultrawave demands a receiver for its very existence. So he could not flash a thought to any

53

of his people unless one of them happened to be listening on that particular "wave"—its pattern of frequency, modulation, and other physical characteristics. And his untrained mind simply did not send on that "band." He couldn't do it, he couldn't imagine the wave-form of his race's normal thought. He was faced with a problem similar to that of a man in a foreign country who must invent its language for himself before he can communicate—without even being allowed to listen to it and knowing only that its phonetic, grammatical, and semantic values are entirely different from those of his native speech.

Insoluble? No, maybe not. His mind lacked the power to send a call out through the stars, lacked the ability to make itself intelligible. But a machine has no such limitations.

He could modify his ultrawave; it already had the power, and he could give it the coherence. For he could insert a random factor in it, a device which would vary the basic wave-form in every conceivable permutation of characteristics, running through millions or billions of tries in a second—and the random wave could be modulated too, his own thoughts could be superimposed. Whenever the machine found resonance with anything that could receive—anything, literally, for millions of light-years—an ultrawave would be generated and the random element cut off. Joel could stay on that band then, examining it at his leisure.

Sooner or later, one of the bands he hit would be that of his race. And he would know it.

* * *

54

The device, when he finished, was crude and ugly, a great ungainly thing of tangled wires and gleaming tubes and swirling cosmic energies. One lead from it connected to a metal band around his own head, imposing his basic ultra-wave pattern on the random factor and feeding back whatever was received into his brain. He lay on his bunk, with a control panel beside him, and started the machine working.

Vague mutterings, sliding shadows, strangeness rising out of the roiled depths of his mind. . . . He grinned thinly, battling down the cold apprehension which rose in his abused nerves, and began experimenting with the machine. He wasn't too sure of all its characteristics himself, and it would take a while too before he had full control of his thought-pattern.

Silence, darkness, and now and then a glimpse, a brief blinding instant when the random gropings struck some basic resonance and a wave sprang into being and talked to his brain. Once he looked through Margaret's eyes, across a table to Langtree's face. There was candlelight, he remembered afterward, and a small string orchestra was playing in the background. Once he saw the ragged outlines of a city men had never built, rising up toward a cloudy sky while a strangely slow and heavy sea leaped against its walls.

Once, too, he did catch a thought flashing between the stars. But it was no thought of his kind, it was a great white blaze like a sun exploding in his head, and cold, cold. He screamed aloud, and for a week afterward dared not resume his experiments.

In the springtime dusk, he found his answer.

The first time, the shock was so great that he lost contact again. He lay shaking, forcing calm on himself, trying to reproduce the exact pattern his own brain, as well as the machine, had been sending. Easy, easy— The baby's mind had been drifting in a mist of dreams, *thus* . . .

The baby. For his groping, uncontrollable brain could not resonate with any of the superbly trained adult minds of his people.

But a baby has no spoken language. Its mind slides amorphously from one pattern to another, there are no habits as yet to fix it, and one tongue is as good as any other. By the laws of randomness, Joel had struck the pattern which an infant of his race happened to be giving out at the moment.

He found it again, and the tingling warmth of contact flowed into him, deliciously, marvelously, a river in a dusty desert, a sun warming the chill of the solipsistic loneliness in which humans wandered from their births to the end of their brief meaningless lives. He fitted his mind to the baby's, let the two streams of consciousness flow into one, a river running toward the mighty sea of the race.

The feral child crept out of the forest. Wolves howled at his back, the hairy four-footed brothers of cave and chase and darkness, but he heard them not. He bent over the baby's cradle, the tangled hair falling past his gaunt witless face, and looked with a dim stirring of awe and wonder. The baby spread its hand, a little soft star-

56

fish, and his own gnarled fingers stole toward it, trembling at the knowledge that this was a paw like his own.

Now he had only to wait until some adult looked into the child's mind. It shouldn't be long, and meanwhile he rested in the timeless drowsy peace of the very young.

Somewhere in the outer cosmos, perhaps on a planet swinging about a sun no one of Earth would ever see, the baby rested in a cradle of warm, pulsing forces. He did not have a room around him, there was a shadowiness which no human could ever quite comprehend, lit by flashes of the energy that created the stars.

The baby sensed the nearing of something that meant warmth and softness, sweetness in his mouth and murmuring in his mind. He cooed with delight, reaching his hands out into the shaking twilight of the room. His mother's mind ran ahead of her, folding about the little one.

A scream!

Frantically, Joel reached for her mind, flashing and flashing the pattern of location-pulses through the baby's brain into hers. He lost her, his mind fell sickeningly in on itself—no, no, someone else was reaching for him now, analyzing the pattern of the machine and his own wild oscillations and fitting smoothly into them.

A deep, strong voice in his brain, somehow unmistakably male— Joel relaxed, letting the other mind control his, simply emitting his signals.

It would take—them—a little while to analyze the meaning of his call. Joel lay in a half-conscious state, aware of one small part of the being's mind maintaining a thread of contact with him while the rest reached out, summoning others across the universe, calling for help and information.

So he had won. Joel thought of Earth, dreamily and somehow wistfully. Odd that in this moment of triumph his mind should swell on the little things he was leaving behind—an Arizona sunset, a nightingale under the moon, Peggy's flushed face bent over an instrument beside his. Beer and music and windy pines.

But O my people! Never more to be lonely ...

Decision. A sensation of falling, rushing down a vortex of stars toward Sol—approach!

The being would have to locate him on Earth. Joel tried to picture a map, though the thought-patterns that corresponded in his brain to a particular visualization would not make sense to the other. But in some obscure way, it might help.

Maybe it did. Suddenly the telepathic band snapped, but there was a rush of other impulses, life forces like flame, the nearness of a god. Joel stumbled gasping to his feet and flung open the door.

The moon was rising above the dark hills, a hazy light over trees and patches of snow and the wet ground. The air was chill and damp, sharp in his lungs.

The being who stood there, outlined in the radiance of his garments, was taller than Joel, an adult. His grave eyes were too brilliant to meet, it was as if the life within him were incandescent. And when the full force of his mind reached out, flowing over and into Joel, running along every nerve and cell of him . . .

He cried out with the pain of it and fell to his hands and knees. The intolerable force lightened, faded to a thrumming in his brain that shook every fiber of it. He was being studied, analyzed, no tiniest part of him was hidden from those terrible eyes and from the logic that recreated more of him than he knew himself. His own distorted telepathic language was at once intelligible to the watcher, and he croaked his appeal.

The answer held pity, but it was as remote and inexorable as the thunders on Olympus.

Child, it is too late. Your mother must have been caught in a –?– energy vortex and caused to –?– on Earth, and now you have been raised by the animals.

Think, child. Think of the feral children of this native race. When they were restored to their own kind, did they become human? No, it was too late. The basic personality traits are determined in the first years of childhood, and their specifically human attributes, unused, had atrophied.

It is too late, too late. Your mind has become too fixed in rigid and limited patterns. Your body has made a different adjustment from that which is necessary to sense and control the forces we use. You even need a machine to speak.

You no longer belong to our race.

Joel lay huddled on the ground, shaking, not thinking or daring to think.

The thunders rolled through his head: *We cannot have you interfering with the proper mental training of our children. And since you can never rejoin your kind, but must make the best adaptation you can to the race you live with, the kindest as well as the wisest thing for us to do is to make certain changes. Your memory and that of others, your body, the work you are doing and have done—*

There were others filling the night, the gods come to Earth, shining and terrible beings who lifted each fragment of experience he had ever had out of him and made their judgments on it. Darkness closed over him, and he fell endlessly into oblivion.

He awoke in his bed, wondering why he should be so tired.

Well, the cosmic-ray research had been a hard and lonely grind. Thank heaven and his lucky stars it was over! He'd take a well-earned vacation at home now. It'd be good to see his friends again—and Peggy.

Dr. Joel Weatherfield, eminent young physicist, rose cheerfully and began making ready to go home.

THE STAR BEAST

CHAPTER I
Therapy for Paradise

THE REBIRTH TECHNICIAN THOUGHT HE HAD HEARD
everything in the course of some three centuries. But he was astonished now.

"My dear fellow—" he said. "Did you say a
tiger—"

"That's right," said Harol. "You can do it,
can't you?"

"Well—I suppose so. I'd have to study the
problem first, of course. Nobody has ever
wanted a rebirth that far from human. But off-
hand I'd say it was possible." The technician's
eyes lit with a gleam which had not been there
for many decades. "It would at least be—
interesting!"

"I think you already have a record of a tiger," said Harol.

"Oh, we must have. We have records of every animal still extant when the technique was invented, and I'm sure there must still have been a few tigers around then. But it's a problem of modification. A human mind just can't exist in a nervous system that different. We'd have to change the record enough—larger brain with more convolutions, of course, and so on .... Even then it'd be far from perfect, but your basic mentality should be stable for a year or two, barring accidents. That's all the time you'd want anyway, isn't it?"

"I suppose so," said Harol.

"Rebirth in animal forms is getting fashionable these days," admitted the technician. "But so far they've only wanted animals with easily modified systems. Anthropoid apes, now—you don't even have to change a chimpanzee's brain at all for it to hold a stable human mentality for years. Elephants are good too. But—a tiger—" He shook his head. "I suppose it can be done, after a fashion. But why not a gorilla?"

"I want a carnivore," said Harol.

"Your psychiatrist, I suppose—" hinted the technician.

Harol nodded curtly. The technician sighed and gave up the hope of juicy confessions. A worker at Rebirth Station heard a lot of strange stories, but this fellow wasn't giving. Oh, well, the mere fact of his demand would furnish gossip for days.

"When can it be ready?" asked Harol.

The technician scratched his head thoughtfully. "It'll take a while," he said. "We have to get the record scanned, you know, and work out a basic neural pattern that'll hold the human mind. It's more than a simple memory-superimposition. The genes control an organism all through its lifespan, dictating, within the limits of environment, even the time and speed of aging. You can't have an animal with an ontogeny entirely opposed to its basic phylogeny—it wouldn't be viable. So we'll have to modify the very molecules of the cells, as well as the gross anatomy of the nervous system."

"In short," smiled Harol, "this intelligent tiger will breed true."

"If it found a similar tigress," answered the technician. "Not a real one—there aren't any left, and besides, the heredity would be too different. But maybe you want a female body for someone?"

"No, I only want a body for myself." Briefly, Harol thought of Avi and tried to imagine her incarnated in the supple, deadly grace of the huge cat. But no, she wasn't the type. And solitude was part of the therapy anyway.

"Once we have the modified record, of course, there's nothing to superimposing your memory patterns on it," said the technician. "That'll be just the usual process, like any human rebirth. But to make up that record—well, I can put the special scanning and computing units over at Research on the problem. Nobody's working there. Say a week. Will that do?"

"Fine," said Harol. "I'll be back in a week."

He turned with a brief good-bye and went down the long slideway toward the nearest transmitter. It was almost deserted now save for the unhuman forms of mobile robots gliding on their errands. The faint, deep hum of activity which filled Rebirth Station was almost entirely that of machines, of electronic flows whispering through vacuum, the silent cerebration of artificial intellects so far surpassing those of their human creators that men could no longer follow their thoughts. A human brain simply couldn't operate with that many simultaneous factors.

The machines were the latter-day oracles. And the life-giving gods. *We're parasites on our machines,* thought Harol. *We're little fleas hopping around on the giants we created, once. There are no real human scientists anymore. How can there be, when the electronic brains and the great machines which are their bodies can do it all so much quicker and better—can do things we would never even have dreamed of, things of which man's highest geniuses have only the faintest glimmer of an understanding? That has paralyzed us, that and the rebirth immortality. Now there's nothing left but a life of idleness and a round of pleasure—and how much fun is anything after centuries?*

It was no wonder that animal rebirth was all the rage. It offered some prospect of novelty—for a while.

He passed a mirror and paused to look at himself. There was nothing unusual about him; he had the tall body and handsome features that were uniform today. There was a little gray at his temples and he was getting a bit bald on top, though this body was only thirty-five. But then

64

it always had aged early. In the old days he'd hardly have reached a hundred.

I am—let me see—four hundred and sixty-three years old. At least, my memory is—and what am I, the essential I, but a memory track?

Unlike most of the people in the building, he wore clothes, a light tunic and cloak. He was a little sensitive about the flabbiness of his body. He really should keep himself in better shape. But what was the point of it, really, when his twenty-year-old record was so superb a specimen?

He reached the transmitter booth and hesitated a moment, wondering where to go. He could go home—have to get his affairs in order before undertaking the tiger phase—or he could drop in on Avi or— His mind wandered away until he came to himself with an angry start. After four and a half centuries, it was getting hard to coordinate all his memories; he was becoming increasingly absent-minded. Have to get the psychostaff at Rebirth to go over his record, one of these generations, and eliminate some of that useless clutter from his synapses.

He decided to visit Avi. As he spoke her name to the transmitter and waited for it to hunt through the electronic files at Central for her current residence, the thought came that in all his lifetime he had only twice seen Rebirth Station from the outside. The place was immense, a featureless pile rearing skyward above the almost empty European forests—as impressive a sight, in its way, as Tycho Crater or the rings of Saturn. But when the transmitter sent you directly from booth to booth, inside the buildings, you rarely had occasion to look at their exteriors.

For a moment he toyed with the thought of having himself transmitted to some nearby house just to see the Station. But—oh, well, any time in the next few millennia. The Station would last forever, and so would he.

The transmitter field was generated. At the speed of light, Harol flashed around the world to Avi's dwelling.

The occasion was ceremonial enough for Ramacan to put on his best clothes, a red cloak over his tunic and the many jeweled ornaments prescribed for formal wear. Then he sat down by his transmitter and waited.

The booth stood just inside the colonnaded verandah. From his seat, Ramacan could look through the open doors to the great slopes and peaks of the Caucasus, green now with returning summer save where the everlasting snows flashed under a bright sky. He had lived here for many centuries, contrary to the restlessness of most Earthlings. But he liked the place. It had a quiet immensity; it never changed. Most humans these days sought variety, a feverish quest for the new and untasted, old minds in young bodies trying to recapture a lost freshness. Ramacan was—they called him stodgy, probably. Stable or steady might be closer to the truth. Which made him ideal for his work. Most of what government remained on Earth was left to him.

Felgi was late. Ramacan didn't worry about it; he was never in a hurry himself. But when the Procyonite did arrive, the manner of it brought an amazed oath even from the Earthling.

He didn't come through the transmitter. He came in a boat from his ship, a lean metal shark drifting out of the sky and sighing to the lawn. Ramacan noticed the flat turrets and the ominous muzzles of guns projecting from them. Anachronism—Sol hadn't seen a warship for more centuries than he could remember. But—

Felgi came out of the airlock. He was followed by a squad of armed guards, who grounded their blasters and stood to stiff attention. The Procyonite captain walked alone up to the house.

Ramacan had met him before, but he studied the man with a new attention. Like most in his fleet, Felgi was a little undersized by Earthly standards, and the rigidity of his face and posture were almost shocking. His severe, form-fitting black uniform differed little from those of his subordinates except for insignia of rank. His features were gaunt, dark with the protective pigmentation necessary under the terrible blaze of Procyon, and there was something in his eyes which Ramacan had never seen before.

The Procyonites looked human enough. But Ramacan wondered if there was any truth to those rumors which had been flying about Earth since their arrival, that mutation and selection during their long and cruel stay had changed the colonists into something that could never have been otherwise.

Certainly their social setup and their basic psychology seemed to be—foreign.

Felgi came up the short escalator to the verandah and bowed stiffly. The psychographs had taught him modern Terrestrial, but his voice still held an echo of the harsh colonial tongue and his phrasing was strange: "Greeting to you, Commander."

Ramacan returned the bow, but his was the elaborate sweeping gesture of Earth. "Be welcome, Gen—ah—General Felgi." Then, informally: "Please come in."

"Thank you." The other man walked into the house.

"Your companions—?"

"My *men* will remain outside." Felgi sat down without being invited, a serious breach of etiquette—but after all, the mores of his home were different.

"As you wish." Ramacan dialed for drinks on the room creator.

"No," said Felgi.

"Pardon me?"

"We don't drink at Procyon. I thought you knew that."

"Pardon me. I had forgotten." Regretfully, Ramacan let the wine and glasses return to the matter bank and sat down.

Felgi sat with steely erectness, making the efforts of the seat to mold itself to his contours futile. Slowly, Ramacan recognized the emotion that crackled and smoldered behind the dark lean visage.

Anger.

"I trust you are finding your stay on Earth pleasant," he said into the silence.

"Let us not make meaningless words," snapped Felgi. "I am here on business."

"As you wish." Ramacan tried to relax, but he couldn't; his nerves and muscles were suddenly tight.

"As far as I can gather," said Felgi, "you head the government of Sol."

"I suppose you could say that. I have the title of Coordinator. But there isn't much to coordinate these days. Our social system practically runs itself."

"Insofar as you have one. But actually you are completely disorganized. Every individual seems to be sufficient to himself."

"Naturally. When everyone owns a matter creator which can supply all his ordinary needs, there is bound to be economic and thus a large degree of social independence. We have public services, of course—Rebirth Station, Power Station, Transmitter Central, and a few others. But there aren't many."

"I cannot see why you aren't overwhelmed by crime." The last word was necessarily Procyonian, and Ramacan raised his eyebrows puzzledly. "Anti-social behavior," explained Felgi irritably. "Theft, murder, destruction."

"What possible need has anyone to steal?" asked Ramacan, surprised. "And the present degree of independence virtually eliminates social friction. Actual psychoses have been removed from the neural components of the rebirth records long ago."

"At any rate, I assume you speak for Sol."

"How can I speak for almost a billion different people? I have little authority, you know.

69

So little is needed. However, I'll do all I can if you'll only tell me—"

"The decadence of Sol is incredible," snapped Felgi.

"You may be right." Ramacan's tone was mild, but he bristled under the urbane surface. "I've sometimes thought so myself. However, what has that to do with the present subject of discussion—whatever it may be?"

"You left us in exile," said Felgi, and now the wrath and hate were edging his voice, glittering out of his eyes. "For nine hundred years, Earth lived in luxury while the humans on Procyon fought and suffered and died in the worst kind of hell."

"What reason was there for us to go to Procyon?" asked Ramacan. "After the first few ships had established a colony there—well, we had a whole galaxy before us. When no colonial ships came from your star, I suppose it was assumed the people there had died off. Somebody should perhaps have gone there to check up, but it took twenty years to get there and it was an inhospitable and unrewarding system and there were so many other stars. Then the matter creator came along and Sol no longer had a government to look after such things. Space travel became an individual business, and no individual was interested in Procyon." He shrugged. "I'm sorry."

"You're *sorry*!" Felgi spat the words out. "For nine hundred years our ancestors fought the bitterness of their planets, starved and died in misery, sank back almost to barbarism and had to slug their way every step back upwards,

70

waged the cruelest war of history with the Czernigi—unending centuries of war until one race or the other should be exterminated. We died of old age, generation after generation of us—we wrung our needs out of planets never meant for humans—my ship spent twenty years getting back here, twenty years of short human lives—and you're sorry!"

He sprang up and paced the floor, his bitter voice lashing out. "You've had the stars, you've had immortality, you've had everything which can be made of matter. And *we* spent twenty years cramped up in metal walls to get here—wondering if perhaps Sol hadn't fallen on evil times and needed our help!"

"What would you have us do now?" demanded Ramacan. "All Earth has made you welcome—"

"We're a novelty!"

"—all Earth is ready to offer you all it can. What more do you want of us?"

For a moment the rage was still in Felgi's strange eyes. Then it faded, blinked out as if he had drawn a curtain across them, and he stood still and spoke with sudden quietness. "True. I—I should apologize, I suppose. The nervous strain—"

"Don't mention it," said Ramacan. But inwardly he wondered. Just how far could he trust the Procyonites? All those hard centuries of war and intrigue—and then they weren't really human anymore, not the way Earth's dwellers were human—but what else could he do? "It's quite all right. I understand."

71

"Thank you." Felgi sat down again. "May I ask what you offer?"

"Duplicate matter creators, of course. And robots duplicated, to administer the more complex Rebirth techniques. Certain of the processes involved are beyond the understanding of the human mind."

"I'm not sure it would be a good thing for us," said Felgi. "Sol has gotten stagnant. There doesn't seem to have been any significant change in the last half millennium. Why, our spaceship drives are better than yours."

"What do you expect?" shrugged Ramacan. "What possible incentive have we for change? Progress, to use an archaic term, is a means to an end, and we have reached its goal."

"I still don't know—" Felgi rubbed his chin. "I'm not even sure how your duplicators work."

"I can't tell you much about them. But the greatest technical mind on Earth can't tell you everything. As I told you before, the whole thing is just too immense for real knowledge. Only the electronic brains can handle so much at once."

"Maybe you could give me a short résumé of it, and tell me just what your setup is. I'm especially interested in the actual means by which it's put to use."

"Well, let me see." Ramacan searched his memory. "The ultrawave was discovered—oh, it must be a good seven or eight hundred years ago now. It carries energy, but it's not electromagnetic. The theory of it, as far as any human can follow it, ties in with wave mechanics.

"The first great application came with the dis-

covery that ultrawaves transmit over distances
of many astronomical units, unhindered by intervening matter, and with *no energy loss*. The
theory of that has been interpreted as meaning
that the wave is, well, I suppose you could say
it's 'aware' of the receiver and only goes to it.
There must be a receiver as well as a transmitter to generate the wave. Naturally, that led to
a perfectly efficient power transmitter. Today
all the Solar System gets its energy from the
Sun—transmitted by the Power Station on the
day side of Mercury. Everything from inter-
planetary spaceships to televisors and clocks
runs from that power source."

"Sounds dangerous to me," said Felgi. "Suppose the station fails?"

"It won't," said Ramacan confidently. "The
Station has its own robots, no human technicians at all. Everything is recorded. If any one
part goes wrong, it is automatically dissolved
into the nearest matter bank and recreated.
There are other safeguards too. The Station has
never given trouble since it was first built."

"I see—" Felgi's tone was thoughtful.

"Soon thereafter," said Ramacan, "it was
found that the ultra-wave could also transmit
matter. Circuits could be built which would
scan any body atom by atom, dissolve it to energy, and transmit this energy on the ultrawave
along with the scanning signal. At the receiver,
of course, the process is reversed. I'm grossly
oversimplifying, naturally. It's not a mere signal which is involved, but a fantastic complex
of signals such as only the ultrawave could
carry. However, you get the general idea. Just

about all transportation today is by this technique. Vehicles for air or space exist only for very special purposes and for pleasure trips."

"You have some kind of controlling center for this too, don't you?"

"Yes. Transmitter Station, on Earth, is in Brazil. It holds all the records of such things as addresses, and it coordinates the millions of units all over the planet. It's a huge, complicated affair, of course, but perfectly efficient. Since distance no longer means anything, it's most practical to centralize the public-service units.

"Well, from transmission it was but a step to recording the signal and reproducing it out of a bank of any other matter. So—the duplicator. The matter creator. You can imagine what that did to Sol's economy! Today everybody owns one, and if he doesn't have a record of what he wants he can have one duplicated and transmitted from Creator Station's great 'library.' Anything whatsoever in the way of material goods is his for the turning of a dial and the flicking of a switch.

"And this, in turn, soon led to the Rebirth technique. It's but an extension of all that has gone before. Your body is recorded at its prime of life, say around twenty years of age. Then you live for as much longer as you care to, say to thirty-five or forty or whenever you begin to get a little old. Then your neural pattern is recorded alone by special scanning units. Memory, as you surely know, is a matter of neural synapses and altered protein molecules, not too difficult to scan and record. This added pattern is superimposed electronically on the record of your twenty-year-old body. Then your own body is used as the matter bank for materializing the pattern in the altered record and—virtually instaneously—your young body is created—but with all the memories of the old! You're immortal!"

"In a way," said Felgi. "But it still doesn't seem right to me. The ego, the soul, whatever you want to call it—it seems as if you lose that. You create simply a perfect copy."

"When the copy is so perfect it cannot be told from the original," said Ramacan, "then what *is* the difference? The ego is essentially a matter of continuity. You, your essential self, are a constantly changing pattern of synapses bearing only a temporary relationship to the molecules that happen to carry the pattern at the moment. It is the design, not the structural material, that is important. And it is the design that we preserve."

"Do you?" asked Felgi. "I seemed to notice a strong likeness among Earthlings."

"Well, since the records can be altered there was no reason for us to carry around crippled or diseased or deformed bodies," said Ramacan. "Records could be made of perfect specimens and *all* ego-patterns wiped from them; then someone else's neural pattern could be superimposed. Rebirth—in a new body! Naturally, everyone would want to match the prevailing beauty standard, and so a certain uniformity has appeared. A different body would of course lead in time to a different personality, man being a psychosomatic unit. But

75

the continuity which is the essential attribute of the ego would still be there."

"Ummm—I see. May I ask how old you are?"

"About seven hundred and fifty. I was middle-aged when Rebirth was established, but I had myself put into a young body."

Felgi's eyes went from Ramacan's smooth, youthful face to his own hands, with the knobby joints and prominent veins of his sixty years. Briefly, the fingers tightened, but his voice remained soft. "Don't you have trouble keeping your memories straight?"

"Yes, but every so often I have some of the useless and repetitious ones taken out of the record, and that helps. The robots know exactly what part of the pattern corresponds to a given memory and can erase it. After, say, another thousand years, I'll probably have big gaps. But they won't be important."

"How about the apparent acceleration of time with age?"

"That was bad after the first couple of centuries, but then it seemed to flatten out, the nervous system adapted to it. I must say, though," admitted Ramacan, "that it as well as lack of incentive is probably responsible for our present static society and general unproductiveness. There's a terrible tendency to procrastination, and a day seems too short a time to get anything done."

"The end of progress, then—of science, of art, of striving, of all which has made man human."

"Not so. We still have our arts and handicrafts and—hobbies, I suppose you could call them. Maybe we don't do so much anymore, but—why should we?"

"I'm surprised at finding so much of Earth gone back to wilderness. I should think you'd be badly overcrowded."

"Not so. The creator and the transmitter make it possible for men to live far apart, in physical distance, and still be in as close touch as necessary. Communities are obsolete. As for the population problem, there isn't any. After a few children, not many people want more. It's sort of, well, unfashionable anyway."

"That's right," said Felgi quietly, "I've hardly seen a child on Earth."

"And of course there's a slow drift out to the stars as people seek novelty. You can send your recording in a robot ship, and a journey of centuries becomes nothing. I suppose that's another reason for the tranquility of Earth. The more restless and adventurous elements have moved away."

"Have you any communication with them?"

"None. Not when spaceships can only go at half the speed of light. Once in a while curious wanderers will drop in on us, but it's very rare. They seem to be developing some strange cultures out in the galaxy."

"Don't you do *any* work on Earth?"

"Oh, some public services must be maintained—psychiatry, human technicians to oversee various stations, and so on. And then there are any number of personal-service enterprises—entertainment, especially, and the creation of intricate handicrafts for the creators to duplicate. But there are enough people willing to work a few hours a month or week, if only to fill their time or to get the credit-balance which will enable them to purchase such services for themselves if they desire.

"It's a perfectly stable culture, General Felgi. It's perhaps the only really stable society in all human history."

"I wonder—haven't you any precautions at all? Any military forces, say defenses against invaders—*anything*?"

"Why in the cosmos should we fear that?" exclaimed Ramacan. "Who would come invading over light-years—at half the speed of light? Or if they did, *why*?"

"Plunder—"

Ramacan laughed. "We could duplicate anything they asked for and give it to them."

"Could you, now?" Suddenly Felgi stood up. "Could you?"

Ramacan rose too, with his nerves and muscles tightening again. There was a hard triumph in the Procyonite's face, vindictive, threatening.

Felgi signaled to his men through the door. They trotted up on the double, and their blasters were raised and something hard and ugly was in their eyes.

"Coordinator Ramacan," said Felgi, "you are under arrest."

"What—what—" The Earthling felt as if someone had struck him a physical blow. He clutched for support. Vaguely he heard the iron tones:

"You've confirmed what I thought. Earth is unarmed, unprepared, helplessly dependent on

78

a few undefended key spots. And I captain a warship of space filled with soldiers.

"We're taking over!"

CHAPTER II
"Tiger, Tiger!"

Avi's current house lay in North America, on the middle Atlantic seaboard. Like most private homes these days, it was small and low-ceilinged, with adjustable interior walls and furnishings for easy variegation. She loved flowers, and great brilliant gardens bloomed around her dwelling, down toward the sea and landward to the edge of the immense forest which had returned with the end of agriculture.

They walked between the shrubs and trees and blossoms, she and Harol. Her unbound hair was long and bright in the sea breeze, her eighteen-year-old form was slim and graceful as a young deer's. Suddenly he hated the thought of leaving her.

"I'll miss you, Harol," she said.

He smiled lopsidedly. "You'll get over that," he said. "There are others. I suppose you'll be looking up some of those spacemen they say arrived from Procyon a few days ago."

"Of course," she said innocently. "I'm surprised you don't stay around and try for some of the women they had along. It would be a change."

79

"Not much of a change," he answered. "Frankly, I'm at a loss to understand the modern passion for variety. One person seems very much the same as another in that regard."

"It's a matter of companionship," she said. "After not too many years of living with someone, you get to know him too well. You can tell exactly what he's going to do, what he'll say to you, what he'll have for dinner and what sort of show he'll want to go to in the evening. These colonists will be—new! They'll have other ways from ours, they'll be able to tell of a new, different planetary system, they'll—" She broke off. "But now so many women will be after the strangers, I doubt if I'll have a chance."

"But if it's conversation you want—oh, well." Harol shrugged. "Anyway, I understand the Procyonites still have family relationships. They'll be quite jealous of their women. And I need this change."

"A carnivore—!" Avi laughed, and Harol thought again what music it was. "You have an original mind, at least." Suddenly she was earnest. She held both his hands and looked close into his eyes. "That's always been what I like about you, Harol. You've always been a thinker and adventurer, you've never let yourself grow mentally lazy like most of us. After we've been apart for a few years, you're always new again, you've gotten out of your rut and done something strange, you've learned something different, you've grown young again. We've always come back to each other, dear, and I've always been glad of it."

"And I," he said quietly. "Though I've regretted the separations too." He smiled, a wry smile with a tinge of sorrow behind it. "We could have been very happy in the old days, Avi. We would have been married and together for life."

"A few years, and then age and feebleness and death." She shuddered. "Death! Nothingness! Not even the world can exist when one is dead. Not when you've no brain left to know about it. Just—nothing. As if you had never been! Haven't you ever been afraid of the thought?"

"No," he said, and kissed her.

"That's another way you're different," she murmured. "I wonder why you never went out to the stars, Harol. All your children did."

"I asked you to go with me, once."

"Not I. I like it here. Life is fun, Harol. I don't seem to get bored as easily as most people. But that isn't answering my question."

"Yes, it is," he said, and then clamped his mouth shut.

He stood looking at her, wondering if he was the last man on Earth who loved a woman, wondering how she really felt about him. Perhaps, in her way, she loved him—they always came back to each other. But not in the way he cared for her, not so that being apart was a gnawing pain and reunion was—No matter.

"I'll still be around," he said. "I'll be wandering through the woods here; I'll have the Rebirth men transmit me back to your house and then I'll be in the neighborhood."

"My pet tiger," she smiled. "Come around to see me once in a while, Harol. Come with me to some of the parties."

A nice spectacular ornament— "No, thanks.

But you can scratch my head and feed me big bloody steaks, and I'll arch my back and purr."

They walked hand in hand toward the beach. "What made you decide to be a tiger?" she asked.

"My psychiatrist recommended an animal rebirth," he replied. "I'm getting terribly neurotic, Avi. I can't sit still five minutes and I get gloomy spells where nothing seems worthwhile anymore, life is a dreadful farce and—well, it seems to be becoming a rather common disorder these days. Essentially it's boredom. When you have everything without working for it, life can become horribly flat. When you've lived for centuries, tried it all hundreds of times—no change, no real excitement, nothing to call forth all that's in you— Anyway, the doctor suggested I go to the stars. When I refused that, he suggested I change to animal for a while. But I didn't want to be like everyone else. Not an ape or an elephant."

"Same old contrary Harol," she murmured, and kissed him. He responded with unexpected violence.

"A year or two of wild life, in a new and unhuman body, will make all the difference," he said after a while. They lay on the sand, feeling the sunlight wash over them, hearing the lullaby of waves and smelling the clean, harsh tang of sea and salt and many windy kilometers. High overhead a gull circled, white against the blue.

"Won't you change?" she asked.

"Oh, yes. I won't ever be able to remember a

lot of things I now know. I doubt if even the most intelligent tiger could understand vector analysis. But that won't matter, I'll get it back when they restore my human form. When I feel the personality change has gone as far as is safe, I'll come here and you can send me back to Rebirth. The important thing is the therapy—a change of viewpoint, a new and challenging environment— Avi!" He sat up, on one elbow and looked down at her. "Avi, why don't you come along? Why don't we both become tigers?"

"And have lots of little tigers?" she smiled drowsily. "No, thanks, Harol. Maybe some day, but not now. I'm really not an adventurous person at all." She stretched, and snuggled back against the warm white dune. "I like it the way it is."

And there are those starmen— Sunfire, what's the matter with me? Next thing you know I'll commit an inurbanity against one of her lovers. I need that therapy, all right.

"And then you'll come back and tell me about it," said Avi.

"Maybe not," he teased her. "Maybe I'll find a beautiful tigress somewhere and become so enamored of her I'll never want to change back to human."

"There won't be any tigresses unless you persuade someone else to go along." she answered. "But will you like a human body after having had such a lovely striped skin? Will we poor hairless people still look good to you?"

"Darling," he smiled, "to me you'll always look good enough to eat."

83

Presently they went back into the house. The sea gull still dipped and soared, high in the sky.

The forest was great and green and mysterious, with sunlight dappling the shadows and a riot of ferns and flowers under the huge old trees. There were brooks tinkling their darkling way between cool, mossy banks, fish leaping like silver streaks in the bright shallows, lonely pools where quiet hung like a mantle, open meadows of wind-rippled grass, space and solitude and an unending pulse of life.

Tiger eyes saw less than human; the world seemed dim and flat and colorless until he got used to it. After that he had increasing difficulty remembering what color and perspective were like. And his other senses came alive, he realized what a captive within his own skull he had been—looking out at a world of which he had never been so real a part as now.

He heard sounds and tones no man had ever perceived, the faint hum and chirr of insects, the rustling of leaves in a light, warm breeze, the vague whisper of an owl's wings, the scurrying of small, frightened creatures through the long grass—it all blended into a rich symphony, the heartbeat and breath of the forest. And his nostrils quivered to the infinite variety of smells, the heady fragrance of crushed grass, the pungency of fungus and decay, the sharp, wild odor of fur, the hot drunkenness of newly spilled blood. And he felt with every hair, his whiskers quivered to the smallest stirrings, he gloried in the deep, strong play of his muscles—he had come alive, he thought; a man was half dead compared to the vitality that throbbed in the tiger.

At night, at night—there was no darkness for him now. Moonlight was a white, cold blaze through which he stole on feathery feet; the blackest gloom was light to him—shadows, wan patches of luminescence, a shifting, sliding fantasy of gray like an old and suddenly remembered dream.

He laired in a cave he found, and his new body had no discomfort from the damp earth. At night he would stalk out, a huge, dim ghost with only the amber gleam of his eyes for light, and the forest would speak to him with sound and scent and feeling, the taste of game on the wind. He was master then, all the woods shivered and huddled away from him. He was death in black and gold.

Once an ancient poem ran through the human part of his mind. He let the words roll like ominous thunder in his brain and tried to speak them aloud. The forest shivered with the tiger's coughing roar.

> *Tiger, tiger, burning bright*
> *In the forests of the night,*
> *What immortal hand or eye*
> *Could frame thy fearful symmetry?*

And the arrogant feline soul snarled response: *I did!*

Later he tried to recall the poem, but he couldn't.

At first he was not very successful, too much of his human awkwardness clung to him. He snarled his rage and bafflement when rabbits skittered aside, when a deer scented him lurking and bolted. He went to Avi's house and she fed him big chunks of raw meat and laughed and scratched him under the chin. She was delighted with her pet.

Avi, he thought, and remembered that he loved her. But that was with his human body. To the tiger, she had no esthetic or sexual value. But he liked to let her stroke him, he purred like a mighty engine and rubbed against her slim legs. She was still very dear to him, and when he became human again—

But the tiger's instincts fought their way back; the heritage of a million years was not to be denied no matter how much the technicians had tried to alter him. They had accomplished little more than to increase his intelligence, and the tiger nerves and glands were still there.

The night came when he saw a flock of rabbits dancing in the moonlight and pounced on them. One huge, steely-taloned paw swooped down, he felt the ripping flesh and snapping bone and then he was gulping the sweet, hot blood and peeling the meat from the frail ribs. He went wild, he roared and raged all night, shouting his exultance to the pale frosty moon. At dawn he slunk back to his cave, wearied, his human mind a little ashamed of it all. But the next night he was hunting again.

His first deer! He lay patiently on a branch overhanging a trail; only his nervous tail moved while the slow hours dragged by, and he waited. And when the doe passed underneath he was on her like a tawny lightning bolt. A great slapping paw, jaws like shears, a brief, terrible struggle, and she lay dead at his feet. He gorged himself, he ate till he could hardly crawl back to the cave, and then he slept like a drunken man until hunger woke him and he went back to the carcass. A pack of wild dogs was devouring it. He rushed on them and killed one and scattered the rest. Thereafter he continued his feast until only bones were left.

The forest was full of game; it was an easy life for a tiger. But not too easy. He never knew whether he would go back with full or empty belly, and that was part of the pleasure.

They had not removed all the tiger memories; fragments remained to puzzle him; sometimes he woke up whimpering with a dim wonder as to where he was and what had happened. He seemed to remember misty jungle dawns, a broad brown river shining under the sun, another cave and another striped form beside him. As time went on he grew confused, he thought vaguely that he must once have hunted sambar and seen the white rhinoceros go by like a moving mountain in the twilight. It was growing harder to keep things straight.

That was, of course, only to be expected. His feline brain could not possibly hold all the memories and concepts of the human, and with the passage of weeks and months he lost the earlier clarity of recollection. He still identified himself with a certain sound, "Harol," and he remembered other forms and scenes—but more and more dimly, as if they were the fading shards of a dream. And he kept firmly in mind that he had to go back to Avi and let her send—

take?—him somewhere else before he forgot who he was.

Well, there was time for that, thought the human component. He wouldn't lose that memory all at once, he'd know well in advance that the superimposed human personality was disintegrating in its strange house and that he ought to get back. Meanwhile he grew more and deeply into the forest life, his horizons narrowed until it seemed the whole of existence.

Now and then he wandered down to the sea and Avi's home, to get a meal and be made much of. But the visits grew more and more infrequent, the open country made him nervous and he couldn't stay indoors after dark.

Tiger, tiger—

And summer wore on.

He woke to a raw wet chill in the cave, rain outside and a mordant wind blowing through dripping dark trees. He shivered and growled, unsheathing his claws, but this was not an enemy he could destroy. The day and the night dragged by in misery.

Tigers had been adaptable beasts in the old days, he recalled; they had ranged as far north as Siberia. But his original had been from the tropics. *Hell!* he cursed, and the thunderous roar rattled through the woods.

But then came crisp, clear days with a wild wind hallooing through a high, pale sky, dead leaves whirling on the gusts and laughing in their thin, dry way. Geese honked in the heavens, southward bound, and the bellowing of stags filled the nights. There was a drunkenness in the air; the tiger rolled in the grass and purred like muted thunder and yowled at the huge orange moon as it rose. His fur thickened, he didn't feel the chill except as a keen tingling in his blood. All his senses were sharpened now, he lived with a knife-edged alertness and learned how to go through the fallen leaves like another shadow.

Indian summer, long lazy days like a resurrected springtime, enormous stars, the crisp smell of rotting vegetation, and his human mind remembered that the leaves were like gold and bronze and flame. He fished in the brooks, scooping up his prey with one hooked sweep; he ranged the woods and roared on the high ridges under the moon.

Then the rains returned, gray and cold and sodden, the world drowned in a wet woe. At night there was frost, numbing his feet and glittering in the starlight, and through the chill silence he could hear the distant beat of the sea. It grew harder to stalk game, he was often hungry. By now he didn't mind that too much, but his reason worried about winter. Maybe he'd better get back.

One night the first snow fell, and in the morning the world was white and still. He plowed through it, growling his anger, and wondered about moving south. But cats aren't given to long journeys. He remembered vaguely that Avi could give him food and shelter.

Avi— For a moment, when he tried to think of her, he thought of a golden, dark-striped body and a harsh feline smell filling the cave above the old wide river. He shook his massive head, angry with himself and the world, and tried to call up her image. The face was dim in his mind, but the scent came back to him, and the low, lovely music of her laughter. He would go to Avi.

He went through the bare forest with the haughty gait of its king, and presently he stood on the beach. The sea was gray and cold and enormous, roaring white-maned on the shore; flying spindrift stung his eyes. He padded along the strand until he saw her house.

It was oddly silent. He went in through the garden. The door stood open, but there was only desertion inside.

Maybe she was away. He curled up on the floor and went to sleep.

He woke much later, hunger gnawing in his guts, and still no one had come. He recalled that she had been wont to go south for the winter. But she wouldn't have forgotten him, she'd have been back from time to time— But the house had little scent of her, she had been away for a long while. And it was disordered. Had she left hastily?

He went over to the creator. He couldn't remember how it worked, but he did recall the process of dialing and switching. He pulled the lever at random with a paw. Nothing happened.

Nothing! The creator was inert.

He roared his disappointment. Slow, puzzled fear came to him. This wasn't as it should be.

But he was hungry. He'd have to try to get his own food, then, and come back later in hopes of finding Avi. He went back into the woods.

Presently he smelled life under the snow.

Bear. Previously, he and the bears had been in a state of watchful neutrality. But this one was asleep, unwary, and his belly cried for food. He tore the shelter apart with a few powerful motions and flung himself on the animal.

It is dangerous to wake a hibernating bear. This one came to with a start, his heavy paw lashed out and the tiger sprang back with blood streaming down his muzzle.

Madness came, a berserk rage that sent him leaping forward. The bear snarled and braced himself. They closed, and suddenly the tiger was fighting for his very life.

He never remembered that battle save as a red whirl of shock and fury, tumbling in the snow and spilling blood to steam in the cold air. Strike, bite, rip, thundering blows against his ribs and skull, the taste of blood hot in his mouth and the insanity of death shrieking and gibbering in his head!

In the end, he staggered bloodily and collapsed on the bear's ripped corpse. For a long time he lay there, and the wild dogs hovered near, waiting for him to die.

After a while he stirred weakly and ate of the bear's flesh. But he couldn't leave. His body was one vast pain, his feet wobbled under him, one paw had been crushed by the great jaws. He lay by the dead bear under the tumbled shelter, and snow fell slowly on them.

The battle and the agony and the nearness of death brought his old instincts to the fore. All tiger, he licked his tattered form and gulped hunks of rotting meat as the days went by and waited for a measure of health to return.

In the end, he limped back toward his cave. Dreamlike memories nagged him; there had been a house and someone who was good but—but—

He was cold and lame and hungry. Winter had come.

Chapter III
Dark Victory

"We have no further use for you," said Felgi, "but in view of the help you've been, you'll be allowed to live—at least till we get back to Procyon and the Council decides your case. Also, you probably have more valuable information about the Solar System than our other prisoners. They're mostly women."

Ramacan looked at the hard, exultant face and answered dully, "If I'd known what you were planning, I'd never have helped."

"Oh, yes, you would have," snorted Felgi. "I saw your reactions when we showed you some of our means of persuasion. You Earthlings are all alike. You've been hiding from death so long that the backbone has all gone out of you. That alone makes you unfit to hold your planet."

"You have the plans of the duplicators and the transmitters and power-beams—all our technology. I helped you get them from the Stations. What more do you want?"

"Earth."

"But why? With the creators and transmitters, you can make your planets like all the old dreams of paradise. Earth is more congenial, yes, but what does environment matter to you now?"

"Earth is still the true home of man," said Felgi. There was a fanaticism in his eyes such as Ramacan had never seen even in nightmare. "It should belong to the best race of man. Also—well, our culture couldn't stand that technology. Procyonite civilization grew up in adversity, it's been nothing but struggle and hardship, it's become part of our nature now. With the Czernigi destroyed, we *must* find another enemy."

Oh, yes, thought Ramacan. *It's happened before, in Earth's bloody old past. Nations that knew nothing but war and suffering became molded by them, glorified the harsh virtues that had enabled them to survive. A militaristic state can't afford peace and leisure and prosperity; its people might begin to think for themselves. So the government looks for conquest outside the borders— Needful or not, there must be war to maintain the control of the military.*

How human are the Procyonites now? What's twisted them in the centuries of their terrible evolution? They're no longer men, they're fighting robots, beasts of prey, they have to have blood.

"You saw us shell the Stations from space," said Felgi. "Rebirth, Creator, Transmitter— they're radioactive craters now. Not a machine is running on Earth, not a tube is alight— nothing! And with the creators on which their

93

lives depended inert, Earthlings will go back to utter savagery."

"Now what?" asked Ramacan wearily.

"We're standing off Mercury, refueling," said Felgi. "Then it's back to Procyon. We'll use our creator to record most of the crew, they can take turns being briefly recreated during the voyage to maintain the ship and correct the course. We'll be little older when we get home.

"Then, of course, the Council will send out a fleet with recorded crews. They'll take over Sol, eliminate the surviving population, and recolonize Earth. After that—" The mad fires blazed high in his eyes. "The stars! A galactic empire, ultimately."

"Just so you can have war," said Ramacan tonelessly. "Just so you can keep your people stupid slaves."

"That's enough," snapped Felgi. "A decadent culture can't be expected to understand our motives."

Ramacan stood thinking. There would still be humans around when the Procyonites came back. There would be forty years to prepare. Men in spaceships, here and there throughout the System, would come home, would see the ruin of Earth and know who must be guilty. With creators, they could rebuild quickly, they could arm themselves, duplicate vengeance-hungry men by the millions.

Unless Solarian man was so far gone in decay that he was only capable of blind panic. But Ramacan didn't think so. Earth had slipped, but not that far.

Felgi seemed to read his mind. There was

cruel satisfaction in his tones: "Earth will have no chance to rearm. We're using the power from Mercury Station to run our own large duplicator, turning rock into osmium fuel for our engines. But when we're finished, we'll blow up the Station too. Spaceships will drift powerless, the colonists on the planets will die as their environmental regulators stop functioning, no wheel will turn in all the Solar System. That, I should think, will be the final touch!"

Indeed, indeed. Without power, without tools, without food or shelter, the final collapse would come. Nothing but a few starveling savages would be left when the Procyonites returned. Ramacan felt an emptiness within himself.

Life had become madness and nightmare. The end. . . .

"You'll stay here till we get around to recording you," said Felgi. He turned on his heel and walked out.

Ramacan slumped back into a seat. His desperate eyes traveled around and around the bare little cabin that was his prison, around and around like the crazy whirl of his thoughts. He looked at the guard who stood in the doorway, leaning on his blaster, contemptuously bored with the captive. If—if— O almighty gods, if *that* was to inherit green Earth!

What to do, what to do? There must be some answer, some way, no problem was altogether without solution. Or was it? What guarantee did he have of cosmic justice? He buried his face in his hands.

I was a coward, he thought. *I was afraid of pain. So I rationalized, I told myself they prob-*

ably didn't want much, I used my influence to help them get duplicators and plans. And the others were cowards too, they yielded, they were cravenly eager to help the conquerors—and this is our pay!

What to do, what to do? If somehow the ship were lost, if it never came back— The Procyonites would wonder. They'd send another ship or two—no more—to investigate. And in forty years Sol could be ready to meet those ships—ready to carry the war to an unprepared enemy—if in the meantime they'd had a chance to rebuild, if Mercury Power Station were spared—

But the ship would blow the Station out of existence, and the ship would return with news of Sol's ruin, and the invaders would come swarming in—would go ravening out through an unsuspecting galaxy like a spreading plague—

How to stop the ship—*now?*

Ramacan grew aware of the thudding of his heart; it seemed to shake his whole body with its violence. And his hands were cold and clumsy, his mouth was parched, he was afraid.

He got up and walked over toward the guard. The Procyonite hefted his blaster, but there was no alertness in him, he had no fear of an unarmed member of the conquered race.

He'll shoot me down, thought Ramacan. *The death I've been running from all my life is on me now. But it's been a long life and a good one, and better to finish it now than drag out a few miserable years as their despised prisoner, and—and—I hate their guts!*

"What do you want?" asked the Procyonite.

"I feel sick," said Ramacan. His voice was almost a whisper in the dryness of his throat. "Let me out."

"Get back."

"It'll be messy. Let me go to the lavatory."

He stumbled, nearly falling. "Go ahead," said the guard curtly. "I'll be along, remember."

Ramacan swayed on his feet as he approached the man. His shaking hands closed on the blaster barrel and yanked the weapon loose. Before the guard could yell, Ramacan drove the butt into his face. A remote corner of his mind was shocked at the savagery that welled up in him when the bones crunched.

The guard toppled. Ramacan eased him to the floor, slugged him again to make sure he would lie quiet, and stripped him of his long outer coat, his boots, and helmet. His hands were really trembling now; he could hardly get the simple garments on.

If he was caught—well, it only made a few minutes' difference. But he was still afraid. Fear screamed inside him.

He forced himself to walk with nightmare slowness down the long corridor. Once he passed another man, but there was no discovery. When he had rounded the corner, he was violently sick.

He went down a ladder to the engine room. Thank the gods he'd been interested enough to inquire about the layout of the ship when they first arrived! The door stood open and he went in.

A couple of engineers were watching the giant creator at work. It pulsed and hummed and throbbed with power, energy from the sun and from dissolving atoms of rocks—atoms recreated as the osmium that would power the ship's engines on the long voyage back. Tons of fuel spilling down into the bins.

Ramacan closed the soundproof door and shot the engineers.

Then he went over to the creator and reset the controls. It began to manufacture plutonium.

He smiled then, with an immense relief, an incredulous realization that he had won. He sat down and cried with sheer joy.

The ship would not get back. Mercury Station would endure. And on that basis, a few determined men in the Solar System could rebuild. There would be horror on Earth, howling chaos, most of its population would plunge into savagery and death. But enough would live, and remain civilized, and get ready for revenge.

Maybe it was for the best, he thought. Maybe Earth really had gone into a twilight of purposeless ease. True it was that there had been none of the old striving and hoping and gallantry which had made man what he was. No art, no science, no adventure—a smug self-satisfaction, and unreal immortality in a synthetic paradise. Maybe this shock and challenge was what Earth needed, to show the starward way again.

As for him, he had had many centuries of life, and he realized now what a deep inward weariness there had been in him. *Death*, he thought, *death is the longest voyage of all. Without death there is no evolution, no real meaning to life, the ultimate adventure has been snatched away.*

There had been a girl once, he remembered, and she had died before the rebirth machines became available. Odd—after all these centuries he could still remember how her hair had rippled in the wind, one day on a high summery hill. He wondered if he would see her.

He never felt the explosion as the plutonium reached critical mass.

Avi's feet were bleeding. Her shoes had finally given out, and rocks and twigs tore at her feet. The snow was dappled with blood.

Weariness clawed at her, she couldn't keep going—but she had to, she had to, she was afraid to stop in the wilderness.

She had never been alone in her life. There had always been the televisors and the transmitters, no place on Earth had been more than an instant away. But the world had expanded into immensity, the machines were dead, there was only cold and gloom and empty white distances. The world of warmth and music and laughter and casual enjoyment was as remote and unreal as a dream.

Was it a dream? Had she always stumbled sick and hungry through a nightmare world of leafless trees and drifting snow and wind that sheathed her in cold through the thin rags of her garments? Or was this a dream, a sudden madness of horror and death?

Death—no, no, no, she couldn't die, she was one of the immortals, she mustn't die!

The wind blew and blew.

Night was falling, winter night. A wild dog bayed, somewhere out in the gloom. She tried to scream, but her throat was raw with shrieking; only a dry croak would come out.

Help me, help me, help me.

Maybe she should have stayed with the man. He had devised traps, had caught an occasional rabbit or squirrel and flung her the leavings. But he looked at her so strangely when several days had gone by without a catch. He would have killed her and eaten her; she had to flee.

Run, run, run— She couldn't run, the forest reached on forever, she was caught in cold and night, hunger and death.

What had happened, what had happened, what had become of the world? What would become of her?

She had liked to pretend she was one of the ancient goddesses, creating what she willed out of nothingness, served by a huge and eternal world whose one purpose was to serve her. Where was that world now?

Hunger twisted in her like a knife. She tripped over a snow-buried log and lay there, trying feebly to rise.

We were too soft, too complacent, she thought dimly. *We lost all our powers, we were just little parasites on our machines. Now we're unfit—*

No! I won't have it! I was a goddess once—

Spoiled brat, jeered the demon in her mind. *Baby crying for its mother. You should be old enough to look after yourself—after all these centuries. You shouldn't be running in circles waiting for a help that will never come, you should be helping yourself, making a shelter, finding nuts and roots, building a trap. But you can't. All the self-reliance has withered out of you.*

No—help, help, help—

Something moved in the gloom. She choked a scream. Yellow eyes glowed like twin fires, and the immense form stepped noiselessly forth.

For an instant she gibbered in a madness of fear, and then sudden realization came and left her gaping with unbelief—then instant eager acceptance.

There could only be one tiger in this forest.

"Harol," she whispered, and climbed to her feet. "Harol."

It was all right. The nightmare was over. Harol would look after her. He would hunt for her, protect her, bring her back to the world of machines that *must* still exist. "Harol," she cried. "Harol, my dear—"

The tiger stood motionless; only his twitching tail had life. Briefly, irrelevantly, remembered sounds trickled through his mind: *"Your basic mentality should be stable for a year or two, baring accidents. . . ."* But the noise was meaningless, it slipped through his brain into oblivion.

He was hungry. The crippled paw hadn't healed well, he couldn't catch game.

Hunger, the most elemental need of all, grinding within him, filling his tiger brain and tiger body until nothing else was left.

He stood looking at the thing that didn't run away. He had killed another a while back—he licked his mouth at the thought.

From somewhere long ago he remembered

that the thing had once been—he had been—he couldn't remember—

He stalked forward.

"Harol," said Avi. There was fear rising horribly in her voice.

The tiger stopped. He knew that voice. He remembered—he remembered—

He had known her once. There was something about her that held him back.

But he was hungry. And his instincts were clamoring in him.

But if only he could remember, before it was too late—

Time stretched into a horrible eternity while they stood facing each other—the lady and the tiger.

SON OF THE SWORD

CHAPTER I

THEY HAD BURIED PHARAOH, AND NOW SHE STOOD alone in the bed-chamber which had been théirs, looking out into the night and wondering how many sunrises remained to her.

He has not come. The thought ran its endless course through her head, something of the weary creak of a shadoof in its monotony. *He has not come. I sent twice, and I have had no word, and now Tutankhamen is in his grave and they don't need me any longer.*

A breeze wandered in from the gardens and she drew it far into her lungs, fighting for steadiness. *I am afraid to die,* she thought drearily.

There was a light step behind her and she whirled around. The wall was hard against her shoulders, she pressed herself to it and heard the drumming of her heart and the broken gasp of her breath. Eie stood within the doorway.

The guttering lamp cast his shadow huge behind him, and other shadows went sliding over walls and ceiling and out of the farther corners. He stood tall and thin in his white robes, and the darkness was like a veil over his gaunt, hooked face. His eyes caught the light in faint glitter.

"You should not be up, gracious lady," he said. He spoke softly, with the hint of an old man's quaver. "You are tired—it has been a hard and grievous day for you."

"What do you want?" she whispered.

"I wished only to see that you were well," he replied. "It has been a heavy day when your beloved husband was entombed. He walks in the fields of Amen now, but indeed you—miss him."

When she made no response, he went on, slowly: "And now I am to rule over Egypt. Strange how the gods work, my lady! It will be hard for me to meet the splendor of your husband."

Splendor! jeered her mind. She thought of poor sick frightened Tutankhamen, coughing bloody slime out of his lungs, and wondered dully if Eie had a sense of humor.

"I also wished to say—one other thing." Eie tugged his scant gray beard. "I understand that the burden of grief will drive one to do strange things. You were not yourself in the first days after Pharaoh's death, and no one would hold you accountable for what you may have done.

Still—gracious lady, it was unwise to write to the Hittite king."

He knew!

"The Hittites are barbarians and enemies," said Eie, as dryly as a lecturing tutor. "It was the old spider Shubbiluliuma their king who had most to do with riving our empire from us in the days of—your father. It is his doing that our armies must even now be fighting in Syria for the life of Egypt. No, you should not have written." He grimaced, meshing his withered face in wrinkles. "A Hittite prince on the throne of Thebes—you would have given yourself to that! It would have been the Hyksos all over again, the outlanders whom your own glorious ancestors battled to drive from Egypt." He shook his head, and the shadow bobbed and distorted itself behind him. "I really cannot understand it, my lady. Even in the time of sorrow, one would have thought you would remember you are of the royal blood of Egypt."

The room was quiet. So quiet. Beyond the doorway was a cavern of shadow, but she caught the glint of light on the spearheads of Eie's Kushite guardsmen. She wondered in a swimming daze whether they would enter now and kill her.

"Fortunately," said the parched old voice, "the Hittite king was unsure, thinking it a trap. He waited until you wrote again, and that letter the guardians of Egypt learned about. He sent a son of his, but holy Amen still watches over Egypt."

She found her voice again, and it was

strangely flat and steady. "The prince is dead. Your agents murdered him on the way."

"He died of fever, my lady. The Hittites were fully satisfied that it was fever. I had the news only yesterday."

"Let it be fever then," she said wearily. "But, Eie, you could do me one service for old times' sake. It was my father, whose name is abominated now, who raised you to power. It was he who married you to Royal Nurse, which is all the claim you have to the throne of Egypt. You were his master of the horse, and received many signs of his favor, and worshipped with him at the shrine of his god who may not be named anymore. You do owe me something."

"Anything you wish, my lady."

"Tell me—use the divining arts of Amen—tell when I can expect a fever to strike me. I would like to know when."

"Gracious lady!" Eie raised skinny hands. "The very thought! Why, it is my constant prayer as of all Egypt that the gods send you life and health and strength—"

She turned her back, suddenly too tired to be much afraid. "Go away," she said.

"My lady, I am wounded that you should think ill of me—"

"Does it make any difference?" she asked tonelessly. "You are a fool, Eie. You are a jointed doll and it is General Horemheb who pulls the strings, and he in turn is but the tool of the priests of Amen. Even as my husband was, even as I was, all good little tools busily tearing down the work of my father. Surely you don't think that any will you might have to keep me alive could change things? No, the priests tolerated Tutankhamen, since he was weak and afraid and made a glittering show. But my only use was to help keep him on the throne, strengthen his claim a little by my direct royal lineage. Now that he is dead, I too have served my purpose, and the last of Akhnaton's seed which they hate can safely be disposed of. Not that I think you even have any will for my safety. No, you are simply too cowardly to say to my face that I am going to die. So please go away."

"My lady—"

She raised her voice. "Guards, the lord Eie is weary. See him to his chambers."

He stood for a moment, wearing his shadows like a cloak, and then he turned on his heel and walked out. She heard the sandaled feet go on down the corridor.

Pepy crept from the little side room where he slept. He had a beaker of wine in his hand. "Drink this, my lady," he said. "You will sleep better."

She drained it in a few gulps. The slave crouched at her feet, watching her. He was from Kush, black as the night outside, but a hunchbacked dwarf. He wore only a loincloth and a great shining dagger, and his teeth gleamed in his flat face.

"If you wish, lady," he said, "the next time the lord Eie comes here I will spring out at him. One sweep of this blade will end his gabble."

"What good would that do?" she asked, and smiled in spite of herself. Pepy was the last thing they had left her. One by one the servants

107

of her father's time had been peeled away from her on some pretext or other, one by one her friends at court had been replaced; but Pepy the dwarf she had kept at every cost, for he was the last being on earth who loved her.

"No use, my friend," she said. "It is too late. Our little plot has miscarried, and now it is only a matter of days. Most likely poison—you cannot taste all my food for me, nor would they scruple to have you die. I was thinking, though, that I might still be able to send you back to Kush."

He laughed. "No, no, my lady, you will not be rid of old Pepy so easily. Was there another, even at home, who had a kind word for the misshapen little blackskin? Did you not buy me to save me from the usual punishment for stealing from my master?" He wagged his big malformed head solemnly. "Oh, I have stolen from you too, my lady, be sure I have. The royal stores would never miss a few pieces of cake or a little beer or some coppers. I owe you too much, for beer and kindness, to leave you now."

She sighed. "Thank you, Pepy. It is cruel of me to let you stay, but—it is lonely here, you know. They are all waiting and watching and whispering, and none dare be friends with one whom Amen has plainly marked for death."

The wine was strong, and she was beginning to feel it, buzzing in her tired brain. "Oh, I tried to hang on to life, for this is a fair world and I cannot look for much favor from any of the gods in the next one. If indeed there is another, which I begin to doubt. But there is not much left to live for now, when all Egypt is become a jail. It will be good to rest."

Pepy leaned forward until his lips were close to her drooping head. "Lady," he whispered with sudden urgency, "would you then like to leave this jail?"

She started to wakefulness and stared at him.

Pepy laughed again, a high chuckle in the still, flickering dark. "Hee-hee! Nobody notices Pepy the dwarf. He is but a little black cockroach scuttling from corner to corner, sitting in the wineshops and drinking himself silly. But he has very big ears. People have often remarked on his elephant's ears."

"Pepy—"

"Listen, my lady. There is a certain man in Thebes at this moment—"

Thoas raised his hand to the wineshop keeper. "Another!" The man scurried over with a bumper of white-headed Egyptian beer. Thoas turned to the girl who nestled against him. "Come, little sister," he said merrily, "drink with me."

"No, no, I have had enough," she laughed. "The room spins like a chariot wheel."

"Drink, I said!" He held the rim to her lips, and she must perforce let the beer in or see it run over her dress.

"That's a good girl." He kissed her, taking his time about it, and took a long swig out of the goblet. "Ahhh! Nefer, long after the pyramids are crumbled to dust and the name of Egypt is forgotten for all else, men will remember and bless her for beer."

Someone plucked at his tunic. He turned his head, scowling, and looked on the face of the hideous black dwarf who often haunted the tavern. "And what do you want?" he snapped.

"Gracious master," whined the little man, "I bring a message for you."

"Bring it in the morning. Now go away."

"It will not wait, my lord. It concerns your ship."

"Eh?" Thoas gripped the twisted shoulder with a force that brought the breath sucking sharply between teeth. "Eh, what is it, speak!"

"In the corner, sir. It is private."

He followed the Kushite and they squatted together, face to face in the raucous dimness. The dwarf's eyeballs gleamed white.

"Now—what's the matter—quickly!"

"I am a slave in the royal house. They call me Pepy."

"Well, what of it? Hurry, or I'll knock it from your teeth."

"My lord, I hear many things. No one notices a slave. And I heard the chief of the city guards talking with his lieutenants today. They said word had reached them that Thoas of Cyprus had something to do with the disappearance of a certain Egyptian ship on the high seas. They meant to take action."

"How do I know you speak truth?" snapped Thoas harshly.

Pepy shrugged. "You must take my word for it, that is all. You must also do a service for my owner in exchange for this information. It will be quite necessary for you to do so, because you will need my owner's help to escape. There are ships downstream to block off your retreat, and this person is the only one whose influence will get you safely by them. They will stop and search all vessels save one which is carrying her."

"Her! Who is she?"

"Not so fast, my lord Thoas. This is the bargain. You will convey this person out of Egypt and see that she arrives safely and honorably at Cyprus. For this you will have the protection of which I spoke. You will also be paid a good sum of treasure, gold and silver and precious stones from the royal house itself."

Thoas scratched his dark head, wondering how far he could trust—anyone. "You are a liar," he said.

"As you will, my lord. When the guards take you in the city, or the ships do on the Nile, you will see. In any case, it is pure truth that you will be well paid for doing this somewhat dangerous service. Can you afford the risk of not believing me? Or can you afford to lose the reward that is offered?"

"Hm." Thoas felt his tensed muscles loosen a trifle as he reached one of the quick decisions which his life had required. It might be a trap of some sort, but that was unlikely. The Egyptians could take him without subterfuge if they wanted to—there was no conceivable reason for their putting him on guard by any tale, false or otherwise.

Someone wanted the use of his ship very badly. And that meant that—she—would be ready to pay well.

"Who is this?" he asked slowly.

"It is the lady Ankhsenamen, daughter of Pharaoh Akhnaton—on whom be peace—and widow of the Tutankhamen they buried only yesterday."

"Hm—hm!" This began to look interesting, and more than a little dangerous. If the young queen wished to flee the land with the first and best pirate she could find, then she was in trouble. And that meant that she could bring all the hounds of Egypt down on his trail—and Thebes lay a long distance from the open sea. On the other hand, there was always some chance that the dwarf spoke truth about his being wanted for robbery.

"How much will you pay?" he asked.

Pepy named a good sum. Thoas laughed with calculated scorn. "Do you expect me to risk worse than death for that? I'd sooner take my chances on fighting through alone. Make it ten times as great, and I might consider it."

"We can perhaps double the amount, my lord, but that is all we can do. Egypt is not as rich a land as it once was."

"Nine times, and not a copper less. Man, this is perilous work. For your kind of pay, I'd rather swim home."

They haggled for some time, and Pepy reflected that the bold sea rover had an excellent business head. He finally settled for a price that he swore, with many sighs and groans and prayers to the lesser gods, was sheerest blood-sucking—and indeed it would be hard to gather so much wealth in a short time without discovery.

"Now," he said at last, "this is what must be done—"

Thebes drowsed in the heat of early afternoon and the streets were almost empty. Here and there a laborer, a beggar, a poor traveler from the desert might lie curled in an alley or doorway; a squad of Mazaiu marched by, the black guardsmen, sunlight hot on their spearheads; someone or other of the multitude of nations gathered in the city slipped past on an errand of his own. But the rest of the town lay quiet under a windless brassy sky, and echoes threw the hollow sound of feet back from blank-walled houses.

It was a nasty business. Thoas felt a little cold in the dancing, flaring day. Thebes was so still, it had withdrawn to its homes and lay watching in shadow. He had been in situations before where swords were blinking and arrows darkening the air, but this walking openly into the house of the enemy was unnerving.

A couple of priests scurried by on slithering sandaled feet, their shaven pates aglisten in the fierce white light. They looked harmless enough, thought the Cretan, but still they were of the lordship in Egypt and it was far to open sea. It was their breed who had outlived Akhnaton and his brave, silly love of all men, they who had thrown the dead Pharaoh's bright god into the dust, they who had made puppets of two successor kings in the last nine or ten years and were now to crown a third. And it was he who— well, too late to go back now.

His party was small, four sailors of his crew

stalking under burdens of great chests which were empty, the veiled figure of the girl Nefer— a hard time he'd had persuading her to this adventure, gold and blows were needed—and then himself. Five men and a frightened girl from the Theban gutters, walking up to the house of Pharaoh! Briefly, his mouth twisted into a wry grin. They'd make a ballad of this in Cyprus, if he ever got back.

Four guardsmen stood before the side gate in the wall around the palace. One slanted his spear across their path as they approached. "What do you want?" he snapped.

"I am a merchant come at the bidding of the lady Ankhsenamen," answered Thoas. Suddenly he was cool, doubts lost in the urgency of the moment, his mind steady over a deep tautness. "I bring some wares for her highness to inspect."

The guards looked suspiciously up and down his outlander's figure. He wore the short Cretan tunic, with a Phrygian cap on his head and a sea-stained blue cloak over his shoulders. Beneath the headgear was a cap of bronze, and a short sword, hidden by the cloak, was slung over his left arm. He smiled with an insolent easiness.

"I have heard of none such—" began the captain unsurely.

"She sent her dwarf—Pepy, did they call him—after me. Where is that little ape? He'll tell you."

As if he had called on one of the lesser devils, Pepy appeared inside the gate. "Aye, aye, this is the man," he said. "Let them in, Ahmes."

"They're no merchant crew by the looks of them," said the captain. "They've seen plenty of fights, and I'll wager they started most of them too."

"Of course we've had to fight!" growled Thoas indignantly. "It's getting so honest seamen can't venture a league from shore without being set on by some of these cursed pirates. When is your precious Pharaoh going to do something to protect decent folk, eh? Now, let me in, I haven't all day to stand and argue."

Ahmes shook a stubborn head. "The lord Eie said to be particularly careful of robbers. These are uncertain times."

"Five men and a woman to rob the queen of all Egypt!" gibed Pepy. "Well, if all the soldiers are of your caliber, Ahmes, I dare say it might be done."

"What does the woman have to do with all this?"

Pepy leered. "She is to show the use of certain foreign—cosmetics, shall we say?"

Ahmes chuckled. "I don't think the lady Akhsenamen need concern herself much over those anymore. However, let them pass, let them pass."

So that was how the wind blew, reflected Thoas as they came in. Well, he might have known it. The hatred of Amen's priesthood for Akhnaton had not died with the man, and now that they had no more use for his daughter, Tutankhamen's wife, they'd be only too pleased to get rid of her.

To be sure, Pharaoh's blood was sacred in Egypt, and to the common people the thought that even a female child of the dynasty should be murdered was the worst of blasphemy. But the knowledge that Ankhsenamen was to be quietly put out of the way was seemingly general in the more sophisticated court, and nobody seemed to care. Truly the old days were gone.

He murmured fiercely to the dwarf: "You lied to me about the guards being on my trail. There was no need for me to do this!"

Pepy shrugged and grinned. "Well, maybe so. But it will be the truth as soon as we're away from the big house, so I didn't really lie. I only anticipated the fact a bit. Hee-hee!"

"Curse you, I can leave now—"

"Try it and see what happens. I'll scream bloody murder, I will. My lady will deny all knowledge of you. They don't treat robbers well in Egypt. No, no, my lord Thoas, best you remain true to us and earn the reward we promised."

The Cretan snarled, reaching for his sword in a brief rage. It flickered out again, was lost in the thrumming tension of his body, and he managed a sour smile. The little man had trapped him very neatly, and now there was nothing to do but go on with the scheme. But if once they got free, and he had Pepy on the seas, that might be another story.

They went through great cool gardens to the house itself. Long and low it stretched behind its columned portico in a dazzling whiteness with flashes of copper and raw gold. But it was built of mud, he knew, and a generation or two of weather could crumble it back into earth. He thought of the timber hall that was his, that his father had built in the wild hills of Cyprus, and of the windy trees and the long slope of mountain down to the sea, salt air and anchored ships and gulls flying overhead. Suddenly Egypt was stifling.

Into the palace, past motionless Nubian guardsmen, down long dim halls where only soft-footed slaves moved in the midday drowse, and to a doorway screened by an arras of rich weave. Pepy went through without ceremony and beckoned the others after him.

"My lady," he said, bowing grotesquely, "this is Thoas the Cretan, whose merchandise you desired to see."

The newcomer halted, staring in slack-jawed amazement, until the dwarf's snicker brought him back to himself. Was this Ankhsenamen, the widow of Pharaoh and the pawn of empire? Why, she was a girl—she was scarce eighteen years of age and lovely to behold. He looked at her slender supple form, the graceful head and the warm golden skin, and remembered that she was the daughter of Nefertiti whose beauty was still unforgotten in Egypt. Suddenly he thought that his mission might have other rewards than those he had bargained for.

As for her, she saw a medium-tall man, strongly built, with close-cropped dark hair framing a scarred brown face—good lines in that face, though it had something of hardness that she was not used to and the light eyes were cold. His men, behind him, were of his stamp, but uncouth and ill-favored, and she wondered with a brief chill if this was the best way after all.

"No time to spare, my lady," said Pepy. "If the gracious lord Eie, may his bones rot in a dunghill, comes doddering in here, we may have some explaining to do. The luck that Horemheb, who can handle things as they should be handled, is in Memphis, will not see us through other perils."

"Yes—" Thoas pulled his gaze from the long black Egyptian eyes of Ankhsenamen. He remembered that there was money involved. "What about the payment?"

"Here." Pepy opened a great chest in the corner, and the filtered sunlight was shattered on gold and silver and precious stones, fire frozen and glittering in the twilight of the room. "Here, fill your precious caskets and be quick about it."

The sailors stooped greedily over and the jewels rattled into their boxes. Thoas turned to the tavern girl Nefer and stripped the veil and the long cloak from her. He handed then to Ankhsenamen with the curt words, "Put these on. We'll pass you off as this wench when we go out."

Nefer was shivering, and there were tears in her eyes. "What of me?" she whispered. "You promised, Thoas, you promised—"

"Be still!" He slapped her, a hard flat smack in the silence of the room, and his gray eyes were scornful. "I told you what to do. Wait here for a while till we're safely gone. Then simply leave. If anyone asks you, say you were visiting a man, one of the palace servants. They'll believe it of the likes of you. But if you're caught, through your blundering or any other reason, they'll flay you alive in the market square and sell your flesh to the cannibals. Now be still!"

She went over into a corner, trying to stop her trembling.

Thoas turned to find Ankhsenamen's grave regard on him. "That was not a good way to treat her," she said.

"Get that outfit on, or by the belly of Isis I'll leave you here too," he snapped. "Before all the gods—women!" He strode over and helped fill the chests of treasure.

Silently, the queen donned the other woman's outer garments and sat down on the bed to wait. Pepy crept over beside her.

Thoas straightened. "Done," he said. "Now we can go."

"Not quite so fast," said Pepy. "Remember, you are a merchant exhibiting your wares. You will haggle over prices, praise the workmanship and purity, call on all your ancestors to witness that your shoddy imitations are better than the goods of Osiris in Amenti. Sit down, my lord, sit down and entertain us with lies about your warlike exploits."

"That dwarf needs his head taken off," growled one of the sailors.

"To look like you, my beauty? Hee-hee!" Pepy squatted at Ankhsenamen's feet and rocked back and forth on his heels. "No, my lord, I do think it better to take your ease for a while. That guardsman Ahmes has a low and very suspicious nature."

Thoas paced restlessly. "You may be right.

119

But watch your tongue, ape. You're not the favored pet of a queen any longer." His eyes swung to Ankhsenamen. "Nor are you the first lady of a petticoat kingdom. As long as you're with me, you're one of the crew and will jump to my word. Otherwise I'll abandon you wherever you are."

She stiffened, and her reply was cold: "The right to discourtesy was not part of your payment, Captain Thoas."

"Curse it, woman, I *am* the captain, and this fool's errand is desperate enough without a female tongue cluttering things up." His teeth flashed in his sun-darkened face, but it was not a merry smile. "Have no fear. If I can, I'll bring you safe to Cyprus, and unmolested save for what slaps may be needed. Though what you'll do there is beyond me."

"I must rely on you to take me to some noble of good manners," she said, and could not hold her voice quite steady.

"That's not the easiest thing to find on Cyprus, but I'll try. I suppose you mean someone who'll put you in his harem without beating you too often."

"I mean a man of honor."

He shrugged. "Very well. An old man."

She would have asked further, but his manner was too hostile. *But what could I expect?* she thought wearily. It was her doing that he stood under a sword.

"I—I am sorry if you—regret this—" she began.

He grinned again, with a little more warmth. "You are nothing of the sort, Akhsenamen. You

120

are only too happy for a chance to get out of this hellhole alive. No matter, I'd have done the same in your place."

"You're in my lady's place now, lord Thoas," leered Pepy.

CHAPTER II

Thoas fell silent, pacing and scowling and starting at every sound from behind the arras. Time dragged leaden before the dwarf rose and said, "I think we can go now."

Ankhsenamen followed close by Thoas, down the long hall and out to the blinding sunlight. They went through the garden, and she breathed deeply of its heavy fragrance. *I will never see you again, I will never walk in your twilight again. The Nile will flow and the land lie green, and I will be dust blowing in an alien country, O my Egypt. Farewell, farewell, farewell.*

The outer wall loomed above them. Folk were stirring now as the sun began to decline, nobles and servants moving along the paths, and she looked away with a haze before her vision. They were all staring at her, every eye in the world drilled at her back and she didn't dare turn around. Any moment the shout would go up, any moment the guardsmen would come running, and still she paced slowly in the company of the sailors. She remembered nightmares, when she had fled and fled through gray shadows—her feet had been weighted so she could scarce move and the drumming hoofs of pursuit had come nearer and nearer until their thunder filled the world and she had woken up crying in the night. Then her mother would come to hold her close, and perhaps her grave-eyed father would be there to murmur in her ear—but they were dead, they were dead, and she couldn't wake up now.

Her eyes fell on Pepy's gleaming black head where he trotted beside her. Poor little dwarf, brave little monster, he was all that remained, he was the last link with a real world in this slowfooted dream. She thought with a sudden shock that Pepy was closer to her heart than Tutankhamen had ever been.

They came up to the gate. "Let us through again," said Pepy.

"What would you go with them for?" yawned Ahmes.

"None of your affair," snapped the dwarf. "Through!"

"Why," grinned the sentry, "you may have stolen somewhat from her highness. I wouldn't trust any outlander with my shadow. Open those chests, men. They seem to weigh more heavily on your shoulders than when you entered."

"Well," said Pepy slowly, "her highness is getting a bit careless these days. She has other things to think about, they say. Thoas, have you any token for these soldiers?"

The Cretan grunted and dug unwillingly into

his purse. Ahmes and the three other guards took his coins with a snigger. "And a look at your woman," said the captain. "A veil and a heavy cloak are a strange sight in Egypt, whose women might as well wear spun glass. I would see what you are hiding so well from other eyes."

"No." Thoas' voice turned flat and cold. "Let us through or there'll be trouble." He flicked open his cloak to show the sword. "We're all armed. Do we go through or shall there be a fight over it?"

Sullenly, Ahmes opened the gate and they passed out. As Ankhenamen went by, the guards captain reached out a sudden hand and pulled her veil off.

He stood for a moment staring into her face, and his mouth dropped loose. With a rasp of metal, Thoas had his sword out. A gleam in the sunlight, and Ahmes stumbled and fell.

Thoas whirled, yanking his blade free, and stabbed it into the face of the nearest sentry. The hideous crunching of bone was lost in a scream.

One of the burly Cretans raised his loaded chest and sent it crashing into the head of another guard. Skull and box burst asunder, and the jewels rolled in blood. Pepy sprang ape-like, his great dagger aflash, to get the last man from the side as he stabbed after one of the sailors.

"Come on!" Thoas clashed his dripping sword home and grabbed the fainting woman by the wrist. "Drop that other box—two men to a chest—run!"

They fled across the broad avenue, six men

and a girl and half the queen's wealth. Such folk as were abroad scattered wildly, yelling. A horn blew in the gardens behind.

"This way!" gasped Pepy.

Down another street, into a narrow stinking alley, through it to a courtyard and out to a labyrinth winding between huddled mud shacks. They thrust into a mass of people, the ragged poor of Thebes, boiling before and behind them. The roar of voices whirled in blind panic. Brutally, they forced a way through the crowd.

A long time later Thoas halted.

Ankhsenamen swayed against his side, and he saw how her face had whitened and how her breast rose and fell with strangled weeping.

Roughly, he grabbed one slim shoulder and shook her. "Walk! Walk, by Minos, and act your part!"

Pepy's voice was thin. "That is no way to treat my lady. She is not used to bloodshed."

"She'd better get used to it, or some of it will be her own. Come on!"

They forced a slow way through the eddying crowds. Thebes had wakened from its slumber and all the city was out on its various business. Merchants cried their sleazy wares from bazaars like caves in the clay-brick walls; porters hurried by, gasping under their loads; beggars and harlots plied their shrill trades; the narrow, twisting streets brawled with life, they were like rivers shouting between grimy walls, and it was heavy work to push through and death came striding behind.

Ankhsenamen pressed close to Thoas, shoved by the mob, shouted at by drunken men. Any instant, she thought sickly, someone would know her, the cry would arise and the soldiers come thundering down on them.

As if he had read her mind, Thoas suddenly lowered his lips to her ear and murmured: "Little fear of being known. The royal folk have always been so far above these people that they can't imagine you without a golden canopy and a regiment of slaves."

She tried to speak, but her throat was too dry and she managed only to nod. He noticed how her hair shone blue-black in the sun. By all the gods, he thought, a tasty wench! And now that he had only half his payment, he could argue that only half his bargain held. But first they had to get out of this rat's-nest city.

Egypt was a strange land, his mind ran on. He had never understood it. It was the queen of the world and its coffer of gold, it was riotous with life, folk laughed more often here than in any other place he knew—Egyptian women were sweet and eager, Egyptian beer was the blood of life. But ever there brooded over it the shadow of death—the pyramids and the Sphinx at Gizeh, the tombs in the Valley of Kings across the river, vile darkness of the mummy-makers' dens, stupefying pillars and colossi built to beast-headed gods, the talon clutch of a priesthood which sucked its living off the fear of oblivion. Akhnaton had let brief light shine over Egypt, and for his pains his monuments were broken and his name cursed and his child hunted through the streets of Thebes.

O father Nile, you flow broad and cool in a glory of green, and there is laughter among your lotuses and Ra the lifegiver swings on shining wings up into the eye of the sun. But crocodiles swim between your weeds eating the corpses of the murdered.

Thoas remembered again the great draughty hall on the heights of Cyprus and the far blue sea and sunlight streaming down windy slopes to shatter in a million pieces on its waves. Aye, it would be good to come home, if ever they did.

The breathing of his burdened men was heavy behind him. That was something else to reckon with. He could not sail as in the old days when Crete's navy had plowed the eastern sea—these were barbarians of Syria and Cyprus and the sweepings of a dozen civilized ports, and if they agreed that it was wrong for him to risk their necks thusly they'd feed him to the fish. And Ankhsenamen—suddenly he hated to think of what would happen to Ankhsenamen.

The same thing as I intended, he reflected wryly. *Only they are robbers and swine, and I am a very fine fellow.*

Coldly, he began to wonder how many of his crew might stand by him if it came to that.

But first—get out of Thebes!

They strode swiftly along the docks, their feet slapping on stone, until they were at the moorings of the Cretan's own ship.

She was a lean black galley carrying some two score hard-souled crewmen. There was a tiny cabin under the narrow poop, and prow and stem curled up in lotus-like figures plated with tarnished silver. Thoas had had a busy morning gathering his men from taverns and bawdy-houses, kicking them into life and sending them to the ship, and a few were still missing. They watched him with sullen eyes—a mixed and ragged band, Cretan and Cyprian and Nubian and Phoenician and indescribable—robbers, paupers, runaway slaves, and all with edged metal at their waists. They were good men in a fight that was plainly to their advantage, but sometimes skippering them was like living with a cageful of leopards.

Thoas jumped lightly from wharf to poop and looked down the ship's half-open hull. "Off we go!" he cried.

A burly Cyprian pushed aft. "And have you sold all our cargo so soon?"

"Indeed," lied Thoas, though it still lay in the warehouses. Even the half of Ankhsenamen's reward was more than he had expected to get from the sale of a plundered Phoenician galley's load. "And a good price, too. You'll all get your share, but now we must be off."

"With no holiday in Thebes?"

"Where is Chorson—are we leaving without Dogtooth—you've forbidden women aboard and here you bring that wench in broad daylight—" The surly mutter ran around the pressing bearded faces.

Thoas stared coldly at them and drew his bloody sword. "There was trouble," he said, hoping too many dock loungers would not overhear. "We got a good price for our wares, and then I saw a chance to get a little additional and took it. But that led to a fight, and now we must clear from Thebes at once."

"And the woman?" demanded the Cyprian. "The woman?"

"She and her attendant, the dwarf, come with us to our home. She bought passage, and is not to be molested by anyone."

"And now we carry paying passengers?" jeered a voice.

Thoas looked around, and the big Nubian Akhmet who was his friend came up to stand beside him with a wicked-bladed ax in one hand.

The captain said quietly, "We sail now."

The crewmen looked at one another, and grumbled in their beards, and remembered other occasions when Thoas used that tone of voice. They turned to their labor.

A light breeze was springing up over the Nile—from the south, praise Minos—and Thoas ordered the sail set. It bellied listlessly, urging the ship slowly out into the great muddy stream, and men went to their places on the rowers' benches and the creak and splash of oars lifted into the air.

The Cretan stood looking over the rail. He took off his bronze cap and let the wind ruffle his sweat-dampened hair and breathed again of its wetness. On either side of the river lay Thebes, sprawling, massive, the hovels of the poor huddled under the arrogant homes of nobles and gods, the hugeness of Amen's sanctuary incredible on the west bank. A haze of smoke and dust veiled the city, and its unending roar was a muted pulsing in his ears. On the west he could see the brutal reaches of the Libyan Mountains, guarding the Valley of Kings where the great of Egypt lay—where he who had been husband to the girl at his side was a pickled corpse sealed into stone and darkness.

On the east was the smaller Arabian range, its heights touched with the long sunset rays and its lower slopes blue with a dusk that crept upward.

They were away. By all the gods, they were away!

He looked at Ankhsenamen. She was desperately weary, trembling a little and with dark circles under her great eyes, but she stood straight and quiet beside him, looking westward to the sun. The breeze ruffled her heavy black hair and the thin white robe she wore.

She was whispering something, and he bent closer to hear. *"Praise unto thee, light of the world, creator of all things, thou who lookest with love on all nations of man and all which is in them, O Aton—"*

He could not keep from exclaiming: "But that was your father's god!"

She looked up at him, and tears blurred her eyes. "Yes, he was the Aton, the one god who is the maker of all the world and loves it all alike, the one who spoke to my father. We worshipped him with songs and laid flowers on his altar, under the sky in the holy city Akhetaton."

"He is forbidden in Egypt now. You have worshipped Amen for—ten years? Can you even remember the god who lived while you were still a little girl?"

"I can remember him, and sometimes I have whispered prayers to him even in Thebes. I worshipped Amen too, and was afraid. But they kill beasts in the darkness of the temples, and there is only a wooden figure worked by the priests." She lifted her shining head. "I will have done with Amen now, and go back to the Aton who was with me long ago."

Thoas shrugged. For himself, he did not care much about the gods one way or another. He paid whatever dues were customary to the deities of whatever land he happened to be in, and sacrificed to Minos for luck on his voyages, but it was more to appease the fears of his men than out of any very strong beliefs of his own.

"You may have the cabin," he said. "It's cluttered up with storage, but you can find yourself some clothes and bedding in one of the chests and make room for slumber. Pepy can sleep outside your door, if you wish, and I will be within call if you should need me."

"And do you think that we can really escape to Cyprus?" she breathed.

"Who knows? It depends on how soon Eie finds you are gone, and how soon he decides you have fled down the river with the Cretan ship that left in such suspicious haste today—and after that, it depends on how fast his men can go, and whether we get a wind or not. He can drive slaves in relays and outrow us two to one, but with a good breeze, or out in the open sea, I'll show my heels to any Egyptian craft afloat. We must try, that is all."

"You are a bitter man," she said after a silence. "But you have not the look of a plain raider. What are you striving for, Thoas?"

"To get back to Cyprus with my head on my shoulders," he snapped, and turned away to oversee the rowers.

* * *

Toward morning the breeze stiffened to a murmuring wind that filled the sail, and Thoas let his weary oarsmen sleep. They'd need their strength later, he thought—perhaps not so very much later if Pharaoh's troops were close behind.

He himself had caught only short naps as they labored through the night, and now he found himself fully awake. He went aft and relieved the steerman, who curled up on the planks with a sigh and was soon lost to the world, and then, save for a lookout in the bows, he seemed to be the only waking soul aboard.

False dawn had glimmered palely and now darkness returned. The moon had set, and only a vaulted sky of grandly wheeling stars lit his way. Here and there a fire glimmered on the unseen banks, but they slid past in silence and it was lost to view. Looking forward along the shadowy length of the hull, he could make out the dim square of sail, and the river gleamed faintly for a fathom or two beyond the sides. He stood alone in the night of the stars and stillness.

Stillness—it was very quiet now that the moon was down. Only the low sad murmur of wind and the lapping of wavelets against the ship broke the hush. The wind was cool and wet, folding itself around him like a moving cloak. He shivered a little beneath his skin. Once in a while the lonely long-drawn howl of a dog or jackal would quaver out and hang for a time in the night and then be lost again; or a crocodile would slap its tail or a hippopotamus break surface with a smack and splash which carried far in the voiceless night.

Someone stirred in the mass of sleeping men, murmured and whimpered in his dreams. It was strange how helpless even the strongest was in that shadow land. Thoas sighed, and the wind took up the little sound into its own blowing.

Someone else moved, came out of the cabin beneath him and stood for a space looking out over the Nile. Couldn't she sleep either?

"Come up here," he said, very softly, and the wind bore it to her with the ripple of water and the creak of planks and ropes. "Come up here and talk to me for a while."

She climbed the short ladder, her white dress vague in the gloom, and came over to where he stood at the steering oar. When she was close, he could discern her face and form, the lineaments muted by shadow.

"Where is your little friend?" he asked, and knew it was the wrong thing to say.

"He sleeps. Poor Pepy, he has been so anxious and worked so hard." She leaned on the rail, not looking at him, staring across the river to the shore that was a blur of darkness. Presently she laughed, a sad little laugh caught up and scattered by the moving airs. "Strange, is it not, that the only friend of the queen of Egypt should be a hunchbacked slave?"

He could not keep back the harsh retort: "And now you feel so sorry for the poor queen."

"No—not much." She drew a little away from him but did not go haughtily off, and he remembered that she was, after all, very young. "But it is lonely, when you have been used to—everything else."

132

"A change," he admitted, with a smile twisting half his mouth. "You may not like it, you know. Anything could happen to you."

"But I would still be alive, Captain Thoas."

"Are you that afraid to die?"

"No—yes—oh, I don't know. My parents thought little about what comes after death, they said the loving Aton would see to us. And then—they died, and the priests of Amen came back." Her voice rose a little, with a small trembling in it. "They would not even let my father lie dead in peace. They took his tired bones from the grave he had chosen and laid him in disgrace with his mother. They let no one speak his name save as 'that criminal of an Akhnaton.' Nothing shall remain to his memory, so that in time he will die even in the next world, he who had nothing but love for all that was in this one. They hinted that if we were not pleasing to the old gods, Tutankhamen and I, we would not be entombed, our souls would wander homeless. . . . Oh, I didn't know what to believe. Was Amen or Aton the false god, or were all gods a lie and this life a brief meaningless accident, or—" She turned her face up to him, and the starlight glittered off tears. "Thoas, what do you believe? What do they say is true in Cyprus?"

He shrugged. "Some say one thing, some say another. As for me, I find enough to do in this world without worrying about any other."

"But when you die, what then?"

"Some have told me one tale, some another, but I have heard nothing from the lips of any who have themselves died. So I will wait and see. I do say this, though, that you Egyptians

133

think too much about the next life. You should cling to this one and enjoy it as best you can and forget about the rest."

"I—suppose so. It was a good life. I tried to keep it." She smiled uncertainly. "I tried so hard that, had I but succeeded, all the course of the world would have been altered."

"Hm?"

She told him how she had written to the Hittite king, as soon as her husband was dead, and offered marriage to any of his sons. "I had seventy days or so while they made Tutankhamen's mummy ready. Thereafter they would have no use for me. But marriage to a daughter of Pharaoh gives some claim to the throne of Egypt. Had old Shubbiluliuma acted at once—" A fierce note: "What might Egypt and Hatti united not have done! What might they not have done!"

He whistled softly. Was this the frightened girl who had nearly fainted during the brawl at the gate? Had this child attempted such a stroke as men would have remembered for ten thousand years?

Pharaoh's daughter—descendant of men who had kicked the Hyksos barbarians out of the realm and conquered Syria and made the nations of Asia tremble—by all the gods, it meant something!

Slowly, he said, "I am sorry, my lady. I misjudged you."

Her laugh was small and uncertain. "Oh, let us forget all that. I am no longer the queen of Egypt, you know. I am no longer anything."

"Aye. Aye, we've all come down in the world."

"You too?" There was a sudden understanding between them.

"In a way. My father was of a noble family in Crete. He fled when the northerners burned Knossos and came to Cyprus, where he mastered a very petty estate. Underchief of a vassal in a backward part of a barbarian land—well, I have never known anything else, except from tales and from seeing the blackened ruins of Cretan cities, so I can hardly make too much complaint."

"But why have you turned—"

"Pirate? Oh, it is a profitable sideline to trading voyages and farming in the thin soil of home. One can't sit forever in the hearth-smoke, you know." His teeth flashed in the dark. "Besides, I am not a pirate at all. I am doing the same thing my illustrious ancestors must have done, the same thing your great-grandfather Amenhotep did in Syria and the Aegean chiefs are doing now on the northern mainland—conquering myself a kingdom. We are only bandits if we fail."

She laughed aloud this time, with the merriment he thought she should never have lost. It was beginning to lighten just a little, a dull gray stealing into the sky and paling the stars, and the deck was wet with dew.

He could see her more clearly, a young and slim and very beautiful being, and suddenly he said: "Ankhsenamen, it should have been plain that I was your enemy. I don't like danger where it can be avoided, and on your account I was forced to risk ship and men and life. And I don't think you liked me much either. But minds have to change. Let's be friends, shall we?"

Her eyes widened. "Thank you," she whispered.

"Tell Pepy," he said with a grin. "I haven't enjoyed the way he's looked at me and felt the edge of his knife."

Presently she yawned, rubbing her eyes like a little girl, and went back to the cabin. Thoas stood by the oar watching the sun rise in whiteness over the great low land of Egypt.

"Good morning, my lord Aton," he said softly. "Good morning."

Traffic began to thicken on the river as the day waxed, barges and dhows and sea-going galleys and boats plying between the little villages and towns which clustered along the banks. The wind fell and Thoas put his protesting men back at the oars. He and Akhmet had to knock down a couple, and he was aware of surly glances following him.

"How long will it take us to reach the sea?" asked Pepy, squatting over a breakfast of the bread and water and dried fish with which Thoas always kept the ship supplied.

"Two or three days from Thebes, perhaps as much as four," answered the Cretan. "Depends on the wind, among other things."

"Hm." Pepy's eyes darted over the heads of the sweating rowers. Akhmet was pacing up and down the catwalk between the benches with a whip in his hand. "Yes, I can imagine what some of the other things are."

Thoas lowered his voice. "I'd almost welcome

an attack from Pharaoh's troops. Then the men would know we have to get out of the country and be with me. As it is, I can't tell them the real reason for our flight, or they'd blame me—not unjustly—for risking their lives without asking their consent on an errand of little profit to them. Someone would be sure to propose turning Ankhsenamen in for a reward, and then there'd be trouble."

"I thought you were the captain here," said Pepy snappishly.

"Only while I can dominate them. These are pirates, man, not your spirit-broken hirelings of the Nile. I'd trade my soul for a crew of the old Cretan navy, but no such thing is to be had these days."

"If we get away," said Pepy, "I'll give something to all the gods, just to be sure that the one who helped us is paid. I'd make a larger offer to a certain little joss who is very powerful, but I left him behind in Thebes."

"Where will you get the means for such a sacrifice? There are a lot of gods, you know, and you'll be poor as a Libyan mouse."

"Oh, you have plenty of cattle, don't you? My lady said you would be our friend."

"Not for that sort of foolishness," rapped Thoas. The dwarf could make him angry at times.

He got up and stalked forward. The day was already hot, he itched with sweat, and flies buzzed around him. Sleeplessness was sandy under his eyelids. And it went so slowly! They crawled over the sun-glaring water, the creak and rattle of oars chewed at his nerves, the banks crept past. Wasn't a wind to be had in this cursed land?

Ankhsenamen came to stand beside him. Her eyes were red, she had been crying, and her voice was low. "We are nearing Akhetaton," she said.

"So?" He was mostly irritated—with her, with the sun and the river and the wallowing ship and the whole blasted world.

"Nothing," she said tonelessly. "I just wanted to say good-bye to it."

The city appeared over the horizon and they went past. Very white and fair was Akhetaton, dreaming between stony cliffs on the banks of father Nile. Coming upstream, Thoas had thought it perhaps the most beautiful city he had ever seen. But it was dead, empty, only a few old men lived a ghostly existence in its hollow streets and soon they would die and the sands would drift in and Akhetaton would be forgotten.

"We had a garden," murmured the girl. "We had many gardens, but I remember this one so well. It was cool and green within high walls, and there were lotuses growing in a small lake where wild ducks swam. We used to walk together in the evening, father and mother and we sisters, and he would feed the birds and a slave would be playing a harp and singing to us. There was more laughter and kindness in Akhetaton than I have ever met since."

Thoas wiped the sweat from his face. A drop had gotten into his eye. It stung.

"So good-bye, Akhetaton, and sleep well," she said. "There was never a fairer city than you, or a fairer dream than you housed. Good-bye, good-bye."

His tongue seemed to snap of itself: "Yes, a pretty notion, this loving kindness for everything that lived and no thought of whether or not it deserved to live. A very bright bubble which could only have grown in the brain of a sick and sheltered child."

She faced him with a sort of horror. "What do you mean?" she whispered. "What do you mean?"

"I mean that Akhnaton failed his country and brought the ruin of Egypt, and it is his fault that we have to flee now with death at our heels." The words were angry, hard and flat on the hot still air. "While he walked in his beautiful gardens and wrote hymns to the sun, Aziru and Shubbiluliuma were peeling his empire from him. I saw Byblos fall, I was a lad there when the enemy was roaring at the gates and the loyal old chief cried to Pharaoh for help. They say that Aziru wrote slanders about him, and that Akhnaton listened to such lies rather than send men who might kill the enemies of his friends. Rather than fail in his love for all mankind, he let those men who loved him be hacked down and their wives and children be sold into slavery. Cities stood ablaze for want of the troops he could have sent. But no, he loved everyone and Aton forbade killing." Thoas grinned nastily. "Though I don't suppose it was wrong to kill the fly that bit Pharaoh, or the cow he ate, or to drag slaves from Kush and Syria to serve his pleasure." He dropped a hand to his sword hilt. "By Minos, Horemheb is the best thing that happened to Egypt in fifty years!"

"Oh—you too—" She began to cry, but fought back the sobs and walked away with lifted head and stiff back.

I suppose it was unfair, thought the Cretan wearily. *I suppose I should ask her pardon. But can't these people see the truth? Will they need their gold and their courtiers all their lives? Curse it, Knossos was a fair city too.*

The sun flamed into noon and waned westerly. Thoas, stalking down the catwalk, caught a solid wave of human stink, sweat and blood and muttered oaths. The unloaded galley went fast, but her speed was dropping little by little as men came still tired to their shifts. There was a smoldering hate in the eyes that followed him.

At midafternoon, the breathless dancing heat lessened with a gust of wind. Out of the north—the north! Thoas groaned and swore.

"As if we hadn't woes enough," he muttered to Akhmet the Nubian. "Will the breeze endure long?"

"I think it will stiffen. See, there are tiny waves on the river."

"Blowing us down hell-road. Stand by for trouble."

Thoas went on to the cabin. Pepy and Ankhsenamen sat together in what little shade it offered, outside the door. Wordlessly, Thoas entered, got helmet and cuirass from a chest, and donned them. When he came out, the dwarf looked at him inquiringly.

"Do you expect the troops so soon?" he asked low-voiced.

"Mutiny, perhaps," answered Thoas. "The men know little save that their lives are in danger through no fault of their own, and that I am driving them like slaves, and now the very wind is their foe. If fighting starts, get into the cabin."

"Will not your appearing in armor provoke the very trouble?" asked Ankhsenamen. Her voice was so quiet he could scarcely hear it, and she did not meet his eyes.

"Better a live troublemaker than a dead peacemaker," grunted Thoas. His unspoken thought ran on between them: *As your father should have known.*

He mounted the deck and stood looking down the long well of the oarsmen. The sun ran in fire off the bronze of his armor; Ankhsenamen turned dazed eyes from him but his burning after-image stayed in her vision. For a moment there was stillness, only the stridulent oars had voice.

Then a man spoke aloud, harsh and angry: "What do you do in metal, Thoas?"

"If I choose to wear armor, it is my affair," answered the captain coldly. "However, it may be that the Egyptians are close behind. We may all have to don our gear soon, unless we can outrow them."

The man stood up on his bench. It was the rebellious Cyprian, Megacles, a big and wrathful man with matted elf-locks plastered to his streaming face. His oar rattled loose in the rowlock and the others broke their rhythm. Men

141

sleeping exhausted between the benches stirred uneasily, sat up and looked blearily around.

"Get back to your work, Megacles," said Thoas.

"Not before I've had some honest answers," replied the Cyprian. "I want to know why we are fleeing this way, and who this woman is you are carrying off, and what reward has been given you. All of us want to know."

They stirred uneasily on the benches, growling, reaching for the knives at their belts, and some glared at Thoas and some at Megacles. The sun wavered in its veil of heat, and the wind mounted, and the ship drifted idly on the river.

"Back to work, you!" Akhmet came down the catwalk with the ax in one hand and the whip in the other. Men snarled up at him out of gaunt, bearded faces, and he held the lash loose.

"No!" Megacles raised his voice. "We aren't your slaves, Thoas, we're free sailors who have a right to some say in our lives. By Attis, men, shall we take any more of his insolence? If he won't at least tell us why we are here, then overboard with him!"

Another sailor rose, and in a sudden hideous dismay Thoas recognized one of the four who had accompanied him to the palace. He had chosen them for trustworthiness and promised them an extra share in the pay, but—

"I was there," said the man. "I know. And we can't escape the death that's behind us, not if we keep on in this crazy way."

"What is it?" roared Megacles, and the mutterings in throats grew to a ragged bellow. "What is it? Tell us, by Attis!"

"She is a nobleman's daughter," cried Thoas, "but she has nothing to do with—"

"Nobleman, hah!" shouted his sailor. "She's the queen of Egypt, men, that's who she is, and all the troops of Pharaoh are out after her!"

There was a moment's silence. They could not grasp the fact at once. They stood like graven devils.

Thoas spoke loudly: "There is great reward in conveying her to safety, more than we could win in a hundred voyages. Whoever is my friend and stands by me now will be rich."

Megacles leaped by on his bench. "Against all Egypt?" he yelled. "Kill this madman, I say, kill him and turn the woman back to Pharaoh for our lives and what he'll pay us!"

Thoas drew his sword and metal was in his call: "Stand by me now, comrades, stand by and help us flee, or surely Pharaoh will flay us all alive!"

Akhmet grinned savagely and swung his ax. The skull of Megacles split like a rotten melon. Swiftly the Nubian sprang back toward the bows as a dozen knives flashed at him.

"To me!" bellowed Thoas. "To me and Akhmet, all who would stay alive!"

A sailor came snarling up the ladder at him. Thoas stabbed him in the breast. Two others seeking to follow were assailed from behind by a couple of Thoas' party, who took stances below the poop.

"Pepy!" shouted Thoas. "Pepy, in the cabin—weapons!"

The dwarf was already there, staggering under a load of swords and shields. A hurled knife gleamed past his head and thunked into the sternpost. Down in the hull, men reached into the chests under the benches for their arms.

"Here—Thoas, here—"

He turned and saw Ankhsenamen handing up a pair of bows and loaded quivers. Briefly, he smiled at her. "Good!" *Well done, daughter of the Amenhoteps!*

Stringing the bow and nocking an arrow, he drew careful aim at the uncertain, swaying mass of the sailors. A mutineer stood up on his bench crying death for Thoas, and tumbled, clawing at the shaft in his throat. A pair of men trying to storm Akhmet's foredeck screamed as the bowstring hummed.

Men were milling warily about, backs to the rails, growling and making passes with their blades but few ready to do battle on either side. A half dozen stood at each end of the ship, committed to the captain.

"Down there, Akhmet!" called Thoas. "Down and smite them!"

He himself leaped to the benches and attacked the nearest mutineer. Bronze flared hot under the sky, banged and rattled and drew shrieks. Thoas and his tight-clustered followers fought their way down the length of the ship to join Akhmet by the mast. Sailors fell in with them as they advanced, including many who had cried mutiny, and even those who fought did so half-heartedly and were swiftly disarmed. In moments they had peace.

Ankhsenamen mounted the poop and looked forward. There was less death than she had thought, but five corpses rolled with the ship and many were wounded. Blood splashed the planks and groaning sounded under the hot mumble of wind. The unpowered galley wallowed and drifted southward.

Thoas came up to her, grinning and wiping his blade. "You did well," he said. "One would have thought you'd been a pirate queen all your life."

"You—I—it was a matter of life and death for me, you know," she whispered, and wished she could add that his death would have meant something to her as well.

"And you can act at such times, as I ought to know by now," he said. "Ankhsenamen, forget my words earlier today—will you?"

She tried to cover her confusion by stammering: "How swiftly you put down the revolt!"

He shrugged. "If those things don't have a chance to get organized, there is only a witless mob which a few determined men can soon disperse. We were using the flats of our swords most of the time." Grimly: "We'll need all our men soon."

"Do you think they will catch us, then?"

"Most likely. With the men tired, and five dead and others hurt, and this damned wind to fight, and—well, Pharaoh's officer can load two hundred troopers on a swift Nile barge and row them in shifts of fifty—twice or thrice ours—and still use them only half as often as we must work. All that has saved us so far has been whatever delay they had in starting the pursuit, and that cannot have been too great."

"And what will happen when they find us?"

"Why, they'll board us, of course, unless

we're mad enough to board them first, and then we'll fight it out hand to hand. Whatever else happened when ships did battle, unless one could somehow set fire to the other?"

"And we cannot do *anything?*"

"I don't know, Ankhsenamen, I cannot say. Perhaps we can slip past them in the dark, if the gods give us till night. Perhaps we should abandon ship altogether and try to get disguised to Memphis and buy passage for Cyprus. Perhaps we should stand and fight and win." Thoas grimaced. "None of it sounds very likely, does it?"

"And if we are caught—"

"You must take your own counsel. As for me, I don't intend to be taken alive."

She nodded, very slowly, and he saw the slim shoulders stiffen. Quietly, she said: "It is not right. Find me a boat and let me wait on the river for them."

"What?" he cried. "You'd leave and go back to—"

"To the same thing that awaits me if I stay with you." She smiled, but he saw the trembling of her lips. "I have nothing to gain by remaining here, and your life—all your lives to lose. Let me go, let me go so you can escape with the treasure and—and remember me, Thoas."

He shook his helmeted head, wonderingly. "I will never understand you, girl," he said. "You stood two kingdoms on their heads, and sailed for open sea with a gang of cutthroat outlaws, and pulled the wealth of Egypt from under Pharaoh's nose to pay your way—and now you would give up what little chance remains, out of comradeship for men who tried to kill you."

Decisively: "But it is no use, my fair one. There is a little matter of some dead palace guards, and the crime we have committed in stealing you away, and all the trouble we have given the king, and all the loot we have from him—oh, he'd be on our tail just the same." He laid a hand on her shoulder and smiled. "No, no, stay with me, girl."

She shivered and crept against the hardness of his breastplate. Gently, he stroked her hair and kissed her on the forehead.

She laughed a little and whispered: "Is that how the Sea People make love?"

He pulled her close, remembered that he was in plain sight of a shipful of red-handed ribalds, and let her go. "Later," he said, softly and gladly. "But not much later, my dear!"

Chapter III

Pepy came grinning up the ladder. "That's captaincy, my lord Thoas!" he said. "That was the way to lead men—if they won't follow you for love, beat some of it into their thick skulls. Hee-hee! Listen to the slave instructing the captain." He squatted on his haunches before them, a black spider in the sunlight. "But what now, eh? How do we get away from our friends?"

"We don't, I think, unless you have a plan," said Thoas.

Pepy scratched his head. "No. No, not a one, my lord, not a one. My poor wits are quite addled with this queasy ship-motion. I can only suggest that we should begin rowing again instead of talking about it."

"Hm, yes. Give the men a moment or two to rest. I was thinking, though. You know Egypt well enough, Pepy. What are our chances of slipping ashore in the guise of plain peasants?"

"Oh, about like the chances of rolling a thousand sixes in dice, one after the other. Think you not that all Egypt will be out for our blood and the reward of Pharaoh? How would you fool even the dullest fellah into taking any of us for his kind? No, I'll die on shipboard, thank you, and then somebody else can eat the fish that eat me. Hee-hee!"

Thoas nodded tiredly. The wind ruffled the plume on his helmet—the wind, the hot dry wind of Egypt, the cursed hell-wind blowing out of the north. "We may as well get started again," he said in dull tones.

"We may outrun them even now, you know," said Pepy. "Or if we must make a battle—well, if you can do as you just did, captain my lord, I will have no complaint. What is it you Cretans call the Apis bull? Minos, yes, you stood and faced them and gored them down like the bull Minos himself."

Thoas let his mind drift back to Cyprus, to the great-horned black cattle that grazed his father's windy upland pastures and to the sacred bullfights which some of the exiled Cretans still held each year. *If one were only a bull, if the rest were men who fled and screamed and went down under hoofs and horns, a bull bearing Ankhsenamen home to Cyprus. . . .*

Of a sudden he stood dead still, and they looked at him without comprehension. Only the girl thought she knew that face, the stare of a man who sees a holy revelation. Her father had borne it, often and often as he came from the temple of Aton—but this was a fiercer god who had revealed himself to Thoas, and she shivered and fingered the amulet at her throat.

"A bull," he muttered. "Aye, aye, by all the gods, a black bull from old Crete!"

"Eh?" said Pepy.

Thoas whirled and shouted for his men. An anchor splashed overboard and metal gleamed anew. But these were carpenter's tools, thought Ankhsenamen dazedly. They were ripping up the cabin and the decks, they were swarming in a confusion of bodies and voices and Thoas went among them like an unleashed whirlwind.

"What is it?" she cried. "Why aren't we fleeing? What are you doing?"

He gave her a glance that was bright with a wild strange merriment. "We're going to fight instead," he called, "and I am building a little temple in the bows—to Minos!"

The long Egyptian day drew to a close. Standing on the remnants of the poop, Thoas saw the sun-disc red and huge in the west, throwing a bridge of light across the water to his ship. The river flowed broad and quiet and almost deserted between its reedy banks; small waves crossed it, ruffled up by the steady north wind against which the galley toiled downstream. Beyond lay the valley of Egypt, flat green land reaching to the horizon and the deserts beyond.

He had a feeling of the straitness of this realm, bordered by wastes of rock and sand, roofed in by the mighty vault of sky. It seemed to him that the soul of a people must come from the landscape that formed their bones and flesh and thoughts. Crete, where the mountains ran down to the sea, had been half wild, gay and reckless, light as a gull flying. But the soul of Egypt was bound between deserts to a mightily rolling river, and it had grown strong and narrow, marching down an endless road that ran to eternity but had no turnings and no byways. It was an ancient and mighty spirit, it was gray in the youth of kingdoms which were now blowing dust and it would still be walking down its road when the empires of today lay wrecked and buried, but it was not the spirit of the Sea People and the dwellers north of the water. It was not his.

Ankhsenamen came to stand beside him where he held the steering oar. He looked at the airy loveliness of her and remembered that she had blood of Asia in her veins and was herself half an alien in this land.

She said nothing for a while, simply stood facing into the wind that flowed around them. Finally she spoke: "You are a terrible man, Thoas. Men will die for I know not how many thousand years to come, because of what you have done today."

"If it works," he shrugged.

"If not, well, we will return to father Nile," she murmured. Her voice remained steady. "Still—Thoas, I am glad that I failed to wed the Hittite prince. And I am not too sorry to leave this country—with you."

He put a hand about hers. "Thank you, my little one. You will be a mother of kings."

She flushed. "Are you sure?" she whispered. "All the doctors in the empire could not make me have a child by Tutankhamen."

"Seeing that he had no children by any in his overly large harem, I think I know where to look for the trouble," he answered dryly.

She sighed. "I hope so. Poor little king! May he sleep well."

"Did you not care for him?"

"Oh, he was kind enough—but sick and weak and frightened. Save for stiff old Horemheb, who is my enemy, you are the only real man I have known, Thoas."

He grinned until she flushed again.

"Ship ho—behind us, captain, behind us!"

Thoas turned and looked south, down the long sun-flaming road of the Nile. A vessel was heaving into view around a jut of land—no, two, one after the other. It was hard to discern much at this distance, but they were plainly big Nile boats, and they were moving fast.

He raised the cry until the air rang with it: "To arms, men, get ready to fight!"

"Oh—" Ankhsenamen shuddered, and he laid an arm about her waist. "Oh, Thoas, are they the soldiers?"

"I don't know." His face set in tight lines. "I don't know, but it seems likely. Get down below this deck, beloved, get down and cover yourself with a shield."

"If they take us—"

"Keep Pepy and his knife by you. He will do you that service at the last." He kissed her, long and hungrily. "Go!"

The sailors were in an uproar as they donned what armor they had, but it was the noise of fighting men and Thoas smiled to hear it. He went among them, placing some at the oars with shields to protect them, letting the rest stand by with weapons in hand. And he raised the sail. It slatted and banged on the yardarm, the ship yawed violently and he brought her around, southward again.

The pursuing vessels were sweeping in close, not a mile away now. Returning to the steering oar, Thoas looked past his own ship to theirs. Aye, aye, this was the enemy. Soldiers crowded the decks, the sunset light fierce on their arms, and the sweeps were moving like spider feet and the royal standard floated from the mastheads.

"Minos," he whispered. "Minos, be with us."

"Row!" bawled Akhmet, and his whip sang. "Row, you bloody knaves!"

The galley leaped ahead, foam springing from her bows, sail strained and oars flashing. Thoas drew his lips back in a grin that was a snarl.

The nearer of the Egyptian craft loomed before him. A voice drifted from its deck, faint against the wind: "Who are you? Halt before you crash!"

"What do you want of us?" shouted Thoas. "Have we any business with you?"

"Stop in the name of the Pharaoh! We want to search you for a fugitive—"

Thoas gripped his oar tighter. There went the last chance of getting by on pure trickery. Not that it had ever been a good one. Now let the Minos bull face Amen of Egypt!

"Halt, halt, you fool—halt!"

Arrows began to fly from the Egyptians, feathered shafts whistling out of the dusking sky to quiver in planks and shields. One of the pirates yelled and cursed and ripped a missile from his arm. Such of them as had bows shot back.

"Row!" howled Akhmet. "Give it to them! Row! Row! Row!"

The nearer vessel was dead ahead and Thoas, remembering other collisions he had seen, needed every nerve in his body to hold the oar steady. As well that the straining rowers couldn't see, he thought briefly. He luffed a little, approaching from broadside.

The arrows were thick around him. Dimly in the gathering twilight, he saw the hailing shafts fall among his men. Ahead, the soldiers of Egypt should have been making ready to grapple and board. But most of them were staring with bewildered horror at the ship which bore straight for them.

Now!

The crash went through the Cyprian galley like a giant's fist. Thoas stumbled and fell; the steering oar kicked at him and the screaming deck-planks rose to smite his ribs. He heard the high snapping of timbers and the shrieks of men, and rose dizzily and looked forward.

153

The Egyptian vessel was lurching aside, already listing as the Nile poured through the breach he had made in the frail hull. He grabbed for his oar again and Akhmet's whip cracked. The sail banged and rattled as they backed water and came about to face the other galley.

Those were not soldiers of the empire for nothing. Their officers raged among them, using their whips, cursing and bellowing. The arrows were like rain, Thoas saw his men hurt and killed even as they pulled free from the wreckage of the first enemy. This had to be fast!

Not enough room to get up speed—but perhaps the other boat could be disabled at least— "Down sail!" he roared. "Down sail!"

The canvas sagged to the deck as someone cut the lines. The pirates howled and threw their weight against the long oars. Slowly, churning the water, they got under way again, bound for their next opponent.

Its captain was a clever man, thought the Cretan grimly. He was bringing his own ship around to face bow on as the galley surged at him. That was the point of strength, if so weak a thing as a wooden ship had any. But—

Thoas put his oar over, feeling the water kick back against him. Forward—forward!

"Port oars—up!"

His men yanked their sweeps inboard, upward, out of the way. Carried by her own speed, the Cyprian craft slid alongside the Egyptian, and its own port oars smashed to kindling before her. Thoas heard the jagged screaming of men whose breasts were being stove in.

Only—

Sunlight flashed hot on the bronze grapples as men hurled them from the enemy deck. The metal bit deep, wood splintered, the attacking galley was held.

"Board them!"

The Egyptian commander sprang even as he shouted, tumbling from the higher deck to land with both feet on a pirate. They went over in a clash of armor, a sword gleamed, and the captain sprang erect with blood running from his weapon.

He was a big man in the trappings of the royal guard. The others who came leaping after him were common troopers, they probably didn't know the true reason for this pursuit—but he did, and now he had them! He stabbed out, catching one of Thoas' men in the throat, turned, and banged aside a spear probing for his guts.

"Cut those grapples!" roared the Cretan.

Akhmet, with two men at his heels, bounded over the rowers' benches. His ax flared, taut-ened ropes sang as he slashed them. An Egyptian lunged for him; he kicked out with one long leg and sent the man stumbling back across the seats.

"Pull!" yelled Thoas above the rising din of combat. "Starboard oars—pull free!"

Slowly the galley wallowed aside, a man's length of muddy water grew between the two vessels—and the Egyptian, with only one bank of sweeps, could not close the gap. But there were nearly as many soldiers aboard now as pirates, fighting like devils near the bow. *And even if we kill them all,* groaned the mind of Thoas, *we'll lose too many of our own folk to escape.*

He jumped from the poop to the catwalk. "After me!" he shouted. "Drive them into the river!"

The Egyptians were gathered now in a tight rank of swords and shields under the foredeck. Dead men sprawled in front of them, and the galley crew drew back with a snarl. Their tall commander whirled his reddened blade over his head.

"Surrender!" he boomed. "Surrender yourselves to the justice of Pharaoh or feed the crocodiles!"

Thoas went among his men, where they stood unsurely on the catwalk and down in the rowers' well. "Archers!" he snapped. "Shoot them down."

An arrow from the Egyptian line grazed his arm, another hummed nastily by his cheek. One of his men stumbled, clawing at the thing in his breast. To stand and fire would be sheer butchery on both sides—and that remaining galley could still come up to them somehow.

"After me!" cried Thoas again, and moved up to the enemy.

A spear scraped off his breastplate. He stabbed after the man who wielded it, felt his sword go home in flesh and ducked low. The blade of another slashed at his arm, he fell to one knee and let it glance from his helmet. Blood ran hot along his face.

Yanking his sword free, he jabbed upward, into a bare leg. The Egyptian stumbled, and Akhmet's shearing ax clove his neck. Thoas drew back a little and rammed his weapon before him. It caught in the frame of a shield. The man behind it chopped at his wrist, and he let go as edged metal whistled by his fingers.

The pirate on his right went down with a spear in his shoulder. Thoas snatched the dropped sword out of the air and went up again. Blows clanged against his blade, and he could hardly move in the press of men.

"Forward!" shouted the Egyptian chief. "Clear the ship!"

His sword danced like a fiend, striking, stabbing, knocking aside the thrusts against him. Another Cyprian toppled under his feet. Thoas felt rather than saw his own ranks waver.

"By Minos!" He stepped over a wounded man and engaged the Egyptian leader. "One of us—"

The bronze clashed together. Thoas felt the blows shiver in metal and back through its own muscles. Beyond the enemy shield, he saw the lean brown face impassive, frowning a little as the man probed for his life. There was a gleam of sweat on the Egyptian's forehead.

Thoas growled and stood where he was, beating aside the thrusts at his neck and face and lower belly, raking in with his own sword. The Egyptian's shield was a barrier from behind which a snake's tongue licked out. Whirr, clang, and sunlight flaming westward!

A sudden idea which was less a thought than an act of blind desperation—Thoas stepped backward. There was a dead hand underfoot, fingers lax on a sword. He picked it up in his left. The Egyptian commander lunged at him.

Thoas swept his right-hand sword in a clumsy arc that hit the shield and twisted it aside just a little. His left blade struck instantly. The blow shocked home.

Gasping, he saw his enemy sink slowly to the deck, spewing his life red on the planks. A soldier yelled and struck. Thoas took the stab on his armored breast and his own arm straightened with death at its end.

"Men of Egypt! Look! Look here, O Pharaoh's warriors, look up here and see what I have!"

The shrilling cut slowly through the fight, men lifted their eyes toward the poop, pirates and troopers halted for a moment, staring at what was up there.

Ankhsenamen stood on the raised deck. The sunset light was a ruddy fire-streak in her dark blowing hair, and it glanced off the tears across her face. Pepy crouched black and monstrous beside her, one arm about her slim waist, the other brandishing his dagger. In the red luminance it seemed to run blood.

"Look well, Egyptians," cried the dwarf. "This is the lady of the royal house, daughter of Pharaoh, whom we are stealing for ransom. We don't mean to harm her—but unless you lay down your arms, she dies and her holy blood is on you!"

They stood there, unmoving, jaws slack, eyes wide and wild in the tired faces. For a moment that thrummed into forever, they stood wondering—the men of Egypt, the common soldiers who knew not that Ankhsenamen was to be brought home to her death—men who understood that it was better to pay for a treasure than have it thrown away by the robbers and evil fall on the land.

A slow mutter went around the unstirring ranks, and one by one their lifted swords and spears began to drop. Their commander could have enlightened them, but he was a corpse rolling on the deck, and they were only plain troopers.

Thoas sprang up on the catwalk. "It is true," he said. "Lay down your arms, and we will set you ashore. We are agents of Hatti who wish only to use the royal lady as a bargaining point. She will come to no harm."

"No, they will not hurt me, if you yield," said Ankhsenamen. With a sudden imperial ring: "I command you!"

And the Egyptians surrendered.

Thoas looked over his crew. He'd lost more than he liked, but there were enough left to man the ship. His orders cracked out: a guard placed over the prisoners, and the rest to the oars. There might be, probably was, another man in Eie's confidence aboard the disabled barge—but he'd take care of that!

He went downstream a good half mile, turned, and bore back on the other vessel, striking it broadside, amidships. The panicked men aboard it shed their armor and swam for shore. Behind them, the barge settled slowly into the water. The pirates released their captives at wading depth, and then they were alone on the river.

Akhmet came bounding up to Thoas where he stood on the poop, heedless of a dozen arrow gashes, laughing like a boy. "We sank them!" he cried. "Oh, my Captain, we sank them!"

"Our own hull?"

"She's banged up, and has sprung a lot of leaks. But nothing we can't caulk, even without careening. Your reinforced bows held up well, Captain. We can get to Cyprus without trouble. And we sank them!"

"And long before any other Egyptians are after us," said Thoas, "we'll be safe at sea."

He grew aware that Ankhsenamen was at his side again, laughing and weeping and clinging to him. He held her close.

After a while he looked over her shoulder, down into the gleeful face of Pepy. "Well," he said, "your wit was not too seasick to save us. And Minos is still the sea god."

"But you are no bull, my lord," chattered the dwarf. "You were not black and clumsy, you hit them with skill, grace, oh, it was a lovely sight!"

"When we get back to Cyprus," said Thoas reflectively, "I'll start building ships which can really do this kind of work. A bronze beak—yes, my small one, you'll be a queen of the Sea People yet."

"Not a bull," repeated Pepy. "A ram, a ring-horned supple ram. Hee-hee! Yes, my lord, one might say you rammed them!"

They began rowing north again, and slipped past Memphis in the dark out to the delta of the Nile. Dawn showed them the sea, and rising out of eastern waters the sun, day-god, the bright and loving Aton.

FLIGHT TO FOREVER

CHAPTER I
No Return

THAT MORNING IT RAINED, A FINE, SUMMERY MIST blowing over the hills and hiding the gleam of the river and the village beyond. Martin Saunders stood in the doorway letting the cool, wet air blow in his face and wondered what the weather would be like a hundred years from now.

Eve Lang came up behind him and laid a hand on his arm. He smiled down at her, thinking how lovely she was with the raindrops caught in her dark hair like small pearls. She didn't say anything; there was no need for it, and he felt grateful for silence.

He was the first to speak. "Not long now, Eve." And then, realizing the banality of it, he smiled. "Only why do we have this airport feeling? It's not as if I'll be gone long."

"A hundred years," she said.

"Take it easy, darling. The theory is foolproof. I've been on time jaunts before, remember? Twenty years ahead and twenty back. The projector works, it's been proven in practice. This is just a little longer trip, that's all."

"But the automatic machines, that went a hundred years ahead, never came back—"

"Exactly. Some damn fool thing or other went wrong with them. Tubes blew their silly heads off, or some such thing. That's why Sam and I have to go, to see what went wrong. We can repair our machine. We can compensate for the well-known perversity of vacuum tubes."

"But why the two of you? One would be enough. Sam—"

"Sam is no physicist. He might not be able to find the trouble. On the other hand, as a skilled mechanic he can do things I never could. We supplement each other." Saunders took a deep breath. "Look, darling—"

Sam Hull's bass shout rang out to them. "All set, folks! Any time you want to go, we can ride!"

"Coming." Saunders took his time, bidding Eve a proper farewell, a little in advance. She followed him into the house and down to the capacious underground workshop.

The projector stood in a clutter of apparatus under the white radiance of fluoro-tubes. It was unimpressive from the outside, a metal cylinder some ten feet high and thirty feet long with the unfinished look of all experimental setups. The outer shell was simply protection for the battery banks and the massive dimensional projector within. A tiny space in the forward end was left for the two men.

Sam Hull gave them a gay wave. His massive form almost blotted out the gray smocked little body of MacPherson. "All set for a hundred years ahead," he exclaimed. "Two thousand seventy-three, here we come!"

MacPherson blinked owlishly at them from behind thick lenses. "It all tests out," he said. "Or so Sam here tells me. Personally, I wouldn't know an oscillograph from a klystron. You have an ample supply of spare parts and tools. There should be no difficulty."

"I'm not looking for any, Doc," said Saunders. "Eve here won't believe we aren't going to be eaten by monsters with stalked eyes and long fangs. I keep telling her all we're going to do is check your automatic machines, if we can find them, and make a few astronomical observations, and come back."

"There'll be people in the future," said Eve.

"Oh, well, if they invite us in for a drink we won't say no," shrugged Hull. "Which reminds me—" He fished a pint out of his capacious coverall pocket. "We ought to drink a toast or something, huh?"

Saunders frowned a little. He didn't want to add to Eve's impression of a voyage into darkness. She was worried enough, poor kid, poor, lovely kid. "Hell," he said, "we've been back to nineteen fifty-three and seen the house standing. We've been ahead to nineteen ninety-three and seen the house standing. Nobody home at either time. These jaunts are too dull to rate a toast."

"Nothing," said Hull, "is too dull to rate a drink." He poured and they touched glasses, a strange little ceremony in the utterly prosaic laboratory. "Bon voyage!"

"Bon voyage." Eve tried to smile, but the hand that lifted the glass to her lips trembled a little.

"Come on," said Hull. "Let's go, Mart. Sooner we set out, the sooner we can get back."

"Sure." With a gesture of decision, Saunders put down his glass and swung toward the machine. "Good-bye, Eve. I'll see you in a couple of hours—after a hundred years or so."

"So long—Martin." She made the name a caress.

MacPherson beamed with avuncular approval.

Saunders squeezed himself into the forward compartment with Hull. He was a big man, long-limbed and wide-shouldered, with blunt, homely features under a shock of brown hair and wide-set gray eyes lined with crow's feet from much squinting into the sun. He wore only the plain blouse and slacks of his work, stained here and there with grease or acid.

The compartment was barely large enough for the two of them, and crowded with instruments—as well as the rifle and pistol they had along entirely to quiet Eve's fears. Saunders swore as the guns got in his way, and closed the door. The clang had in it an odd note of finality.

"Here goes," said Hull unnecessarily.

Saunders nodded and started the projector warming up. Its powerful thrum filled the cabin and vibrated in his bones. Needles flickered across gauge faces, approaching stable values.

Through the single porthole he saw Eve waving. He waved back and then, with an angry motion, flung down the main switch.

The machine shimmered, blurred, and was gone. Eve drew a shuddering breath and turned back to MacPherson.

Grayness swirled briefly before them, and the drone of the projectors filled the machine with an enormous song. Saunders watched the gauges, and inched back the switch which controlled their rate of time advancement. A hundred years ahead—less the number of days since they'd sent the first automatic, just so that no dunderhead in the future would find it and walk off with it. . . .

He slapped down the switch and the noise and vibration came to a ringing halt.

Sunlight streamed in through the porthole. "No house?" asked Hull.

"A century is a long time," said Saunders. "Come on, let's go out and have a look."

They crawled through the door and stood erect. The machine lay in the bottom of a half-filled pit above which grasses waved. A few broken shards of stone projected from the earth. There was a bright blue sky overhead, with fluffy white clouds blowing across it.

"No automatics," said Hull, looking around.

"That's odd. But maybe the ground-level adjustments—let's go topside." Saunders scrambled up the sloping walls of the pit.

It was obviously the half-filled basement of the old house, which must somehow have been destroyed in the eighty years since his last visit. The ground-level machine in the projector automatically materialized it on the exact surface whenever it emerged. There would be no sudden falls or sudden burials under risen earth. Nor would there be disastrous materializations inside something solid; mass-sensitive circuits prevented the machine from halting whenever solid matter occupied its own space. Liquid or gas molecules could get out of the way fast enough.

Saunders stood in tall, wind-rippled grass and looked over the serene landscape of upper New York State. Nothing had changed, the river and the forested hills beyond it were the same, the sun was bright and clouds shone in the heavens.

No—no, before God! Where was the village?

House gone, town gone—what had happened? Had people simply moved away, or. . . .

He looked back down to the basement. Only a few minutes ago—a hundred years in the past—he had stood there in a tangle of battered apparatus, and Doc and Eve—and now it was a pit with wild grass covering the raw earth. An odd desolation tugged at him.

Was *he* still alive today? Was—Eve? The gerontology of 1973 made it entirely possible, but one never knew. And he didn't want to find out.

"Must'a given the country back to the Indians," grunted Sam Hull.

The prosaic wisecrack restored a sense of balance. After all, any sensible man knew that things changed with time. There would be good and evil in the future as there had been in the past. "—And they lived happily ever after" was pure myth. The important thing was change, an unending flux out of which all could come. And right now there was a job to do.

They scouted around in the grass, but there was no trace of the small automatic projectors. Hull scowled thoughtfully. "You know," he said, "I think they started back and blew out on the way."

"You must be right," nodded Saunders. "We can't have arrived more than a few minutes after their return-point." He started back toward the big machine. "Let's take our observation and get out."

They set up their astronomical equipment and took readings on the declining sun. Waiting for night, they cooked a meal on a camp stove and sat while a cricket-chirring dusk deepened around them.

"I like this future," said Hull. "It's peaceful. Think I'll retire here—or now—in my old age."

The thought of transtemporal resorts made Saunders grin. But—who knew? Maybe!

The stars wheeled grandly overhead. Saunders jotted down figures on right ascension, declination and passage times. From that, they could calculate later, almost to the minute, how far the machine had taken them. They had not moved in space at all, of course, relative to the surface of the earth. "Absolute space" was an obsolete fiction, and as far as the projector was concerned Earth was the immobile center of the universe.

They waded through dew-wet grass back down to the machine. "We'll try ten-year stops, looking for the automatics," said Saunders. "If we don't find 'em that way, to hell with them. I'm hungry."

2063—it was raining into the pit.

2053—sunlight and emptiness.

2043—the pit was fresher now, and a few rotting timbers lay half buried in the ground.

Saunders scowled at the meters. "She's drawing more power than she should," he said.

2023—the house had obviously burned, charred stumps of wood were in sight. And the projector had roared with a skull-cracking insanity of power; energy drained from the batteries like water from a squeezed sponge; a resistor was beginning to glow.

They checked the circuits, inch by inch, wire by wire. Nothing was out of order.

"Let's go." Hull's face was white.

It was a battle to leap the next ten years, it took half an hour of bawling, thundering, tortured labor for the projector to fight backward. Radiated energy made the cabin unendurably hot.

2013—the fire-blackened basement still stood. On its floor lay two small cylinders, tarnished with some years of weathering.

"The automatics got a little further back," said Hull. "Then they quit, and just lay here."

Saunders examined them. When he looked up from his instruments, his face was grim with the choking fear that was rising within him.

"Drained," he said. "Batteries completely dead. They used up all their energy reserves."

"What in the devil is this?" It was almost a snarl from Hull.

"I—don't—know. There seems to be some kind of resistance which increases the further back we try to go—"

"Come on!"

"But—"

"Come on, God damn it!"

Saunders shrugged hopelessly.

It took two hours to fight back five years. Then Saunders stopped the projector. His voice shook.

"No go, Sam. We've used up three quarters of our stored energy—and the farther back we go, the more we use per year. It seems to be some sort of high-order exponential function."

"So—"

"So we'd never make it. At this rate, our batteries will be dead before we get back another ten years." Saunders looked ill. "It's some effect the theory didn't allow for, some accelerating increase in power requirements the farther back into the past we go. For twenty-year hops or less, the energy increases roughly as the square of the number of years traversed. But it must actually be something like an exponential curve, which starts building up fast and furious beyond a certain point. We haven't enough power left in the batteries!"

"If we could recharge them—"

"We don't have such equipment with us. But maybe—"

They climbed out of the ruined basement and

looked eagerly towards the river. There was no sign of the village. It must have been torn down or otherwise destroyed still further back in the past at a point they'd been through.

"No help there," said Saunders.

"We can look for a place. There must be people somewhere!"

"No doubt." Saunders fought for calm. "But we could spend a long time looking for them, you know. And—" His voice wavered. "Sam, I'm not sure even recharging at intervals would help. It looks very much to me as if the curve of energy consumption is approaching a vertical asymptote."

"Talk English, will you?" Hull's grin was forced.

"I mean that beyond a certain number of years an infinite amount of energy may be required. Like the Einsteinian concept of light as the limiting velocity. As you approach the speed of light, the energy needed to accelerate increases ever more rapidly. You'd need infinite energy to get beyond the speed of light—which is just a fancy way of saying you can't do it. The same thing may apply to time as well as space."

"You mean—we can't ever get back?"

"I don't know." Saunders looked desolately around at the smiling landscape. "I could be wrong. But I'm horribly afraid I'm right."

Hull swore. "What're we going to do about it?"

"We've got two choices," Saunders said. "One, we can hunt for people, recharge our batteries, and keep trying. Two, we can go into the future."

"The future!"

"Uh-huh. Sometime in the future, they ought to know more about such things than we do. They may know a way to get around this effect. Certainly they could give us a powerful enough engine so that, if energy is all that's needed, we can get back. A small atomic generator, for instance."

Hull stood with bent head, turning the thought over in his mind. There was a meadowlark singing somewhere, maddeningly sweet.

Saunders forced a harsh laugh. "But the very first thing on the agenda," he said, "is breakfast."

Chapter II
Belgotai of Syrtis

The food was tasteless. They ate in a heavy silence, choking the stuff down. But in the end they looked at each other with a common resolution.

Hull grinned and stuck out a hairy paw. "It's a hell of a roundabout way to get home," he said, "but I'm for it."

Saunders clasped hands with him, wordlessly. They went back to the machine.

"And now where?" asked the mechanic.

"It's two thousand eight," said Saunders. "How about—well—two thousand five hundred A.D.?"

"Okay. It's a nice round number. Anchors aweigh!"

The machine thrummed and shook. Saunders was gratified to notice the small power consumption as the years and decades fled by. At that rate, they had energy enough to travel to the end of the world.

Eve, Eve, I'll come back. I'll come back if I have to go ahead to Judgment Day. . . .

2500 A.D. The machine blinked into materialization on top of a low hill—the pit had filled in during the intervening centuries. Pale, hurried sunlight flashed through wind-driven rain clouds into the hot interior.

"Come," said Hull. "We haven't got all day." He picked up the automatic rifle.

"What's the idea?" exclaimed Saunders.

"Eve was right the first time," said Hull grimly. "Buckle on that pistol, Mart."

Saunders strapped the heavy weapon to his thigh. The metal was cold under his fingers.

They stepped out and swept the horizon. Hull's voice rose in a shout of glee. "People!"

There was a small town beyond the river, near the site of old Hudson. Beyond it lay fields of ripening grain and clumps of trees. There was no sign of a highway. Maybe surface transportation was obsolete now.

The town looked—odd. It must have been there a long time, the houses were weathered. They were tall peak-roofed buildings, crowding narrow streets. A flashing metal tower reared some five hundred feet into the lowering sky, near the center of town.

Somehow, it didn't look the way Saunders

had visualized communities of the future. It had an oddly stunted appearance, despite the high buildings and—sinister? He couldn't say. Maybe it was only his depression.

Something rose from the center of the town, a black ovoid that whipped into the sky and lined out across the river. *Reception committee*, thought Saunders. His hand fell on his pistol butt.

It was an airjet, he saw as it neared, an egg-shaped machine with stubby wings and a flaring tail. It was flying slowly now, gliding groundward toward them.

"Hallo, there!" bawled Hull. He stood erect with the savage wind tossing his flame-red hair, waving. "Hallo, people!"

The machine dove at them. Something stabbed from its nose, a line of smoke—tracers!

Conditioned reflex flung Saunders to the ground. The bullets whined over his head, exploding with a vicious crash behind him. He saw Hull blown apart.

The jet rushed overhead and banked for another assault. Saunders got up and ran, crouching low, weaving back and forth. The line of bullets spanged past him again, throwing up gouts of dirt where they hit. He threw himself down again.

Another try . . . Saunders was knocked off his feet by the bursting of a shell. He rolled over and hugged the ground, hoping the grass would hide him. Dimly, he thought that the jet was too fast for strafing a single man; it overshot its mark.

He heard it whine overhead, without daring

to look up. It circled vulture-like, seeking him. He had time for a rising tide of bitter hate.

Sam—they'd killed him, shot him without provocation—Sam, red-haired Sam with his laughter and his comradeship, Sam was dead and they had killed him.

He risked turning over. The jet was settling to earth; they'd hunt him from the ground. He got up and ran again.

A shot wailed past his ear. He spun around, the pistol in his hand, and snapped a return shot. There were men in black uniforms coming out of the jet. It was long range, but his gun was a heavy war model; it carried. He fired again and felt a savage joy at seeing one of the black-clad figures spin on its heels and lurch to the ground.

The time machine lay before him. No time for heroics; he had to get away—fast! Bullets were singing around him.

He burst through the door and slammed it shut. A slug whanged through the metal wall. Thank God the tubes were still warm!

He threw the main switch. As vision wavered, he saw the pursuers almost on him. One of them was aiming something like a bazooka.

They faded into grayness. He lay back, shuddering. Slowly, he grew aware that his clothes were torn and that a metal fragment had scratched his hand.

And Sam was dead. Sam was dead.

He watched the dial creep upward. Let it be 3000 A.D. Five hundred years was not too much to put between himself and the men in black.

* * *

He chose nighttime. A cautious look outside revealed that he was among tall buildings with little if any light. Good!

He spent a few moments bandaging his injury and changing into the extra clothes Eve had insisted on providing—a heavy wool shirt and breeches, boots and a raincoat that should help make him relatively inconspicuous. The holstered pistol went along, of course, with plenty of extra cartridges. He'd have to leave the machine while he reconnoitered and chance its discovery. At least he could lock the door.

Outside, he found himself standing in a small cobbled courtyard between high houses with shuttered and darkened windows. Overhead was utter night, the stars must be clouded, but he saw a vague red glow to the north, pulsing and flickering. After a moment, he squared his shoulders and started down an alley that was like a cavern of blackness.

Briefly, the incredible situation rose in his mind. In less than an hour he had leaped a thousand years past his own age, had seen his friend murdered and now stood in an alien city more alone than man had ever been. *And Eve, will I see you again?*

A noiseless shadow, blacker than the night, slipped past him. The dim light shone greenly from its eyes—an alley cat. At least man still had pets. But he could have wished for a more reassuring one.

Noise came from ahead, a bobbing light flashing around at the doors of houses. He dropped a hand through the slit in his coat to grasp the pistol butt.

Black against the narrowed skyline four men came abreast, filling the street. The rhythm of their footfalls was military. A guard of some kind. He looked around for shelter; he didn't want to be taken prisoner by unknowns.

No alleys to the side—he sidled backward. The flashlight beam darted ahead, crossed his body, and came back. A voice shouted something, harsh and peremptory.

Saunders turned and ran. The voice cried again behind him. He heard the slam of boots after him. Someone blew a horn, raising echoes that hooted between the high dark walls.

A black form grew out of the night. Fingers like steel wires closed on his arm, yanking him to one side. He opened his mouth, and a hand slipped across it. Before he could recover balance, he was pulled down a flight of stairs in the street.

"In heah." The hissing whisper was taut in his ear. "Quickly."

A door slid open just a crack. They burst through, and the other man closed it behind them. An automatic lock clicked shut.

"Ih don' tink dey vised us," said the man grimly. "Dey better not ha'!"

Saunders stared at him. The other man was of medium height, with a lithe, slender build shown by the skin-tight gray clothes under his black cape. There was a gun at one hip, a pouch at the other. His face was sallow, with a yellowish tinge, and the hair was shaven. It was a lean, strong face, with high cheekbones and narrow jaw, straight nose with flaring nostrils, dark, slant eyes under Mephistophelean brows. The mouth, wide and self-indulgent, was drawn into a reckless grin that showed sharp white teeth. Some sort of white-Mongoloid half-breed, Saunders guessed.

"Who are *you*?" he asked roughly.

The stranger surveyed him shrewdly. "Belgotai of Syrtis," he said at last. "But yuh don' belong heah."

"I'll say I don't." Wry humor rose in Saunders. "Why did you snatch me that way?"

"Yuh didn' wanna fall into de Watch's hands, did yuh?" asked Belgotai. "Don' ask mih why Ih ressued a stranger. Ih happened to come out, see yuh running, figgered anybody running fro de Watch desuhved help, an' pulled yuh back in." He shrugged. "Of course, if yuh don' wanna be helped, go back upstaiahs."

"I'll stay here, of course," he said. "And—thanks for rescuing me."

"*De nada*," said Belgotai. "Come, le's ha' a drink."

It was a smoky, low-ceilinged room, with a few scarred wooden tables crowded about a small charcoal fire and big barrels in the rear—a tavern of some sort, an underworld hangout. Saunders reflected that he might have done worse. Crooks wouldn't be as finicky about his antecedents as officialdom might be. He could ask his way around, learn.

"I'm afraid I haven't any money," he said. "Unless—" He pulled a handful of coins from his pocket.

Belgotai looked sharply at them and drew a whistling breath between his teeth. Then his face smoothed into blankness. "Ih'll buy," he said genially. "Come, Hennaly, gi' us whissey."

Belgotai drew Saunders into a dark corner seat, away from the others in the room. The landlord brought tumblers of rotgut remotely akin to whiskey, and Saunders gulped his with a feeling of need.

"Wha' name do yuh go by?" asked Belgotai.

"Saunders. Martin Saunders."

"Glad to see yuh. Now—" Belgotai leaned closer, and his voice dropped to a whisper— "Now, Saunders, *when* 're yuh from?"

Saunders started. Belgotai smiled thinly. "Be frank," he said. "Dese're mih frien's heah. Dey'd think nawting of slitting yuh troat and dumping yuh in de alley. But Ih mean well."

With a sudden great weariness, Saunders relaxed. What the hell, it had to come out sometime. "Nineteen hundred seventy-three," he said.

"Eh? De future?"

"No—the past."

"Oh. Diff'ent chronning, den. How far back?"

"One thousand and twenty-seven years."

Belgotai whistled. "Long ways! But Ih were sure yuh mus' be from de past. Nobody eve' come fro' de future."

Sickly: "You mean—it's impossible?"

"Ih do' know." Belgotai's grin was wolfish. "Who'd visit dis era fro' de future, if dey could? But wha's yuh story?"

Saunders bristled. The whiskey was coursing hot in his veins now. "I'll trade information," he said coldly. "I won't give it."

"Faiah enawff. Blast away, Mahtin Saundahs."

Saunders told his story in a few words. At the end, Belgotai nodded gravely. "Yuh ran into de Fanatics, five hundred yeahs ago," he said. "Dey was deat' on time travelers. Or on most people, for dat matter."

"But what's happened? What sort of world is this, anyway?"

Belgotai's slurring accents were getting easier to follow. Pronunciation had changed a little, vowels sounded different, the "r" had shifted to something like that in twentieth-century French or Danish, other consonants were modified. Foreign words, especially Spanish, had crept in. But it was still intelligible. Saunders listened. Belgotai was not too well versed in history, but his shrewd brain had a grasp of the more important facts.

The time of troubles had begun in the twenty-third century with the revolt of the Martian colonists against the increasingly corrupt and tyrannical Terrestrial Directorate. A century later the folk of Earth were on the move, driven by famine, pestilence and civil war, a chaos out of which rose the religious enthusiasm of the Armageddonists—the Fanatics, as they were called later. Fifty years after the massacres on Luna, Huntry was the military dictator of Earth, and the rule of the Armageddonists endured for nearly three hundred years. It was a nominal sort of rule, vast territories were always in revolt and the planetary colonists were building up a power which kept the Fanatics out of space, but wherever they did have control they ruled with utter ruthlessness.

Among other things they forbade was time travel. But it had never been popular with anyone since the Time War, when a defeated Directorate army had leaped from the twenty-third to the twenty-fourth century and wrought havoc before their attempt at conquest was smashed. Time travelers were few anyway, the future was too precarious—they were apt to be killed or enslaved in one of the more turbulent periods.

In the late twenty-seventh century, the Planetary League and the African Dissenters had finally ended Fanatic rule. Out of the postwar confusion rose the Pax Africana, and for two hundred years man had enjoyed an era of comparative peace and progress which was wistfully looked back on as a golden age; indeed, modern chronology dated from the ascension of John Mteza I. Breakdown came through internal decay and the onslaughts of barbarians from the outer planets, the Solar System split into a multitude of small states and even independent cities. It was a hard, brawling period, not without a brilliance of its own, but it was drawing to a close now.

"Dis is one of de city-states," said Belgotai. "Liung-Wei, it's named—founded by Sinese invaders about tree centuries ago. It's under de dictatorship of Krausmann now, a stubborn old buzzard who'll no surrender dough de armies of de Atlantic Master're at ouah very gates now. Yuh see de red glow? Dat's deir projectors working on our energy screen. When dey break it down, day'll take de city and punish it for holding out so long. Nobody looks happily to dat day."

He added a few remarks about himself. Belgotai was of a dying age, the past era of small states who employed mercenaries to fight their battles. Born on Mars, Belgotai had hired out over the whole Solar System. But the little mercenary companies were helpless before the organized levies of the rising nations, and after the annihilation of his band Belgotai had fled to Earth where he dragged out a weary existence as thief and assassin. He had little to look forward to.

"Nobody wants a free comrade now," he said ruefully. "If de Watch don't catch me first, Ih'll hang when de Atlantics take de city."

Saunders nodded with a certain sympathy.

Belgotai leaned close with a gleam in his slant eyes. "But yuh can help me, Mahtin Saundahs," he hissed. "And help yuhself too."

"Eh?" Saunders blinked wearily at him.

"Sure, sure. Take me wid yuh, out of dis damned time. Dey can't help yuh here, dey know no more about time travel dan yuh do—most likely dey'll trow yuh in de calabozo and smash yuh machine. Yuh have to go on. Take me!"

Saunders hesitated, warily. What did he really know? How much truth was in Belgotai's story? How far could he trust—"

"Set me off in some time when a free comrade can fight again. Meanwhile Ih'll help. Ih'm a good man wid gun or vibrodagger. Yuh can't go batting alone into de future."

Saunders wondered. But what the hell—it was plain enough that this period was of no use to him. And Belgotai had saved him, even if the Watch wasn't as bad as he claimed. And—well—he needed someone to talk to, if nothing else. Someone to help him forget Sam Hull and the gulf of centuries separating him from Eve.

Decision came. "Okay."

"Wonnaful! Yuh'll no be sorry, Mahtin." Belgotai stood up. "Come, le's be blasting off."

"Now?"

"De sooner de better. Someone may find yuh machine. Den it's too late."

"But—you'll want to make ready—say goodbye—"

Belgotai slapped his pouch. "All Ih own is heah." Bitterness underlay his reckless laugh. "Ih've none to say good-bye to, except mih creditors. Come!"

Half dazed, Saunders followed him out of the tavern. This time-hopping was going too fast for him, he didn't have a chance to adjust.

For instance, if he ever got back to his own time he'd have descendants in this age. At the rate at which lines of descent spread, there would be men in each army who had his own and Eve's blood, warring on each other without thought of the tendernesss which had wrought their very beings. But then, he remembered wearily, he had never considered the common ancestors he must have with men he'd shot out of the sky in the war he once had fought.

Men lived in their own times, a brief flash of light ringed with an enormous dark, and it was not in their nature to think beyond that little span of years. He began to realize why time travel had never been common.

"Hist!" Belgotai drew him into the tunnel of an alley. They crouched there while four black-caped men of the Watch strode past. In the wan red light, Saunders had a glimpse of high cheekbones, half-Oriental features, the metallic gleam of guns slung over their shoulders.

They made their way to the machine where it lay between lowering houses crouched in a night of fear and waiting. Belgotai laughed again, a soft, joyous ring in the dark. "Freedom!" he whispered.

They crawled into it and Saunders set the controls for a hundred years ahead. Belgotai scowled. "Most like de world'll be very tame and quiet den," he said.

"If I get a way to return," said Saunders, "I'll carry you on whenever you want to go."

"Or yuh could carry me back a hundred years from now," said the warrior. "Blast away, den!"

3100 A.D. A waste of blackened, fused rock. Saunders switched on the Geiger counter and it clattered crazily. Radioactive! Some hellish atomic bomb had wiped Liung-Wei from existence. He leaped another century, shaking.

3200 A.D. The radioactivity was gone, but the desolation remained, a vast vitrified crater under a hot, still sky, dead and lifeless. There was little prospect of walking across it in search of man, nor did Saunders want to get far from the machine. If he should be cut off from it. . . .

By 3500, soil had drifted back over the ruined land and a forest was growing. They stood in a drizzling rain and looked around them.

"Big trees," said Saunders. "This forest has

stood for a long time without human interference."

"Maybe man went back to de caves?" suggested Belgotai.

"I doubt it. Civilization was just too widespread for a lapse into total savagery. But it may be a long ways to a settlement."

"Le's go ahead, den!" Belgotai's eyes gleamed with interest.

The forest still stood for centuries thereafter. Saunders scowled in worry. He didn't like this business of going farther and farther from his time, he was already too far ahead ever to get back without help. Surely, in all ages of human history—

4100 A.D. They flashed into materialization on a broad grassy sward where low, rounded buildings of something that looked like tinted plastic stood between fountains, statues, and bowers. A small aircraft whispered noiselessly overhead, no sign of motive power on its exterior.

There were humans around, young men and women who wore long colorful capes over light tunics. They crowded forward with a shout. Saunders and Belgotai stepped out, raising hands in a gesture of friendship. But the warrior kept his hands close to his gun.

The language was a flowing, musical tongue with only a baffling hint of familiarity. Had times changed that much?

They were taken to one of the buildings. Within its cool, spacious interior, a grave, bearded man in ornate red robes stood up to greet them. Someone else brought in a small machine reminiscent of an oscilloscope with microphone attachments. The man set it on the table and adjusted its dials.

He spoke again, his own unknown language rippling from his lips. But words came out of the machine—English!

"Welcome, travelers, to this branch of the American College. Please be seated."

Saunders and Belgotai gaped. The man smiled. "I see the psychophone is new to you. It is a receiver of encephalic emissions from the speech centers. When one speaks, the corresponding thoughts are taken by the machine, greatly amplified, and beamed to the brain of the listener, who interprets them in terms of his own language.

"Permit me to introduce myself. I am Hamalon Avard; dean of this branch of the College." He raised bushy gray eyebrows in polite inquiry.

They gave their names and Avard bowed ceremoniously. A slim girl, whose scanty dress caused Belgotai's eyes to widen, brought a tray of sandwiches and a beverage not unlike tea. Saunders suddenly realized how hungry and tired he was. He collapsed into a seat that molded itself to his contours and looked dully at Avard.

Their story came out, and the dean nodded. "I thought you were time travelers," he said. "But this is a matter of great interest. The archaeology departments will want to speak to you, if you will be so kind—"

"Can you help us?" asked Saunders bluntly. "Can you fix our machine so it will reverse?"

"Alas, no. I am afraid our physics holds no hope for you. I can consult the experts, but I am sure there has been no change in spatiotemporal theory since Priogan's reformulation. According to it, the energy needed to travel into the past increases tremendously with the period covered. The deformation of world lines, you see. Beyond a period of about seventy years, infinite energy is required."

Saunders nodded dully. "I thought so. Then there's no hope?"

"Not in this time, I am afraid. But science is advancing rapidly. Contact with alien culture in the Galaxy has proved an immense stimulant—"

"Yuh have interstellar travel?" exploded Belgotai. "Yuh can travel to de stars?"

"Yes, of course. The faster-than-light drive was worked out over five hundred years ago on the basis of Priogan's modified relativity theory. It involves warping through higher dimensions—But you have more urgent problems than scientific theories."

"Not Ih!" said Belgotai fiercely. "If Ih can get put among de stars—dere must be wars dere—"

"Alas, yes, the rapid expansion of the frontier has thrown the Galaxy into chaos. But I do not think you could get passage on a spaceship. In fact, the Council will probably order your temporal deportation as unintegrated individuals. The sanity of Sol will be in danger otherwise."

"Why, yuh—" Belgotai snarled and reached for his gun. Saunders clapped a hand on the warrior's arm.

"Take it easy, you bloody fool," he said furiously. "We can't fight a whole planet. Why should we? There'll be other ages."

Belgotai relaxed, but his eyes were still angry.

They stayed at the College for two days. Avard and his colleagues were courteous, hospitable, eager to hear what the travelers had to tell of their periods. They provided food and living quarters and much-needed rest. They even pleaded Belgotai's case to the Solar Council, via telescreen. But the answer was inexorable: the Galaxy already had too many barbarians. The travelers would have to go.

Their batteries were taken out of the machine for them and a small atomic engine with nearly limitless energy reserves installed in its place. Avard gave them a psychophone for communication with whoever they met in the future. Everyone was very nice and considerate. But Saunders found himself reluctantly agreeing with Belgotai. He didn't care much for these overcivilized gentlefolk. He didn't belong in this age.

Avard bade them grave good-bye. "It is strange to see you go," he said. "It is a strange thought that you will still be traveling long after my cremation, that you will see things I cannot dream of." Briefly, something stirred in his face. "In a way I envy you." He turned away quickly, as if afraid of the thought. "Good-bye and good fortune."

4300 A.D. The campus buildings were gone, but small, elaborate summerhouses had replaced them. Youths and girls in scanty rainbow-hued dress crowded around the machine.

"You are time travelers?" asked one of the young men, wide-eyed.

Saunders nodded, feeling too tired for speech.

"Time travelers!" A girl squealed in delight.

"I don't suppose you have any means of traveling into the past these days?" asked Saunders hopelessly.

"Not that I know of. But please come, stay for a while, tell us about your journeys. This is the biggest lark we've had since the ship came from Sirius."

There was no denying the eager insistence. The women, in particular, crowded around, circling them in a ring of soft arms, laughing and shouting and pulling them away from the machine. Belgotai grinned. "Le's stay de night," he suggested.

Saunders didn't feel like arguing the point. There was time enough, he thought bitterly. All the time in the world.

It was a night of revelry. Saunders managed to get a few facts. Sol was a Galactic backwater these days, stuffed with mercantile wealth and guarded by nonhuman mercenaries against the interstellar raiders and conquerors. This region was one of many playgrounds for the children of the great merchant families, living for generations off inherited riches. They were amiable kids, but there was a mental and physical softness over them, and a deep inward weariness from a meaningless round of increasingly stale pleasure. Decadence.

Saunders finally sat alone under a moon that

glittered with the diamond-points of domed cities, beside a softly lapping artificial lake, and watched the constellations wheel overhead—the far suns that man had conquered without mastering himself. He thought of Eve and wanted to cry, but the hollowness in his breast was dry and cold.

CHAPTER III
Trapped in the Time-Stream

Belgotai had a thumping hangover in the morning which a drink offered by one of the women removed. He argued for a while about staying in this age. Nobody would deny him passage this time; they were eager for fighting men out in the Galaxy. But the fact that Sol was rarely visited now, that he might have to wait years, finally decided him on continuing.

"Dis won' go on much longer," he said. "Sol is too tempting a prize, an' mercenaries aren' allays loyal. Sooner or later, dere'll be war on Eart' again."

Saunders nodded dispiritedly. He hated to think of the blasting energies that would devour a peaceful and harmless folk, the looting and murdering and enslaving, but history was that way. It was littered with the graves of pacifists.

The bright scene swirled into grayness. They drove ahead.

4400 A.D. A villa was burning, smoke and flame reaching up into the clouded sky. Behind it stood the looming bulk of a ray-scarred spaceship, and around it boiled a vortex of men, huge bearded men in helmets and cuirasses, laughing as they bore out golden loot and struggling captives. The barbarians had come!

The two travelers leaped back into the machine. Those weapons could fuse it to a glowing mass. Saunders swung the main-drive switch far over.

"We'd better make a longer jump," Saunders said, as the needle crept past the century mark. "Can't look for much scientific progress in a dark age. I'll try for five thousand A.D."

His mind carried the thought on: *Will there ever be progress of the sort we must have? Eve, will I ever see you again?* As if his yearning could carry over the abyss of millennia: *Don't mourn me too long, my dearest. In all the bloody ages of human history, your happiness is all that ultimately matters.*

As the needle approached six centuries, Saunders tried to ease down the switch. Tried!

"What's the matter?" Belgotai leaned over his shoulder.

With a sudden cold sweat along his ribs, Saunders tugged harder. The switch was immobile—the projector wouldn't stop.

"Out of order?" asked Belgotai anxiously.

"No—it's the automatic mass-detector. We'd be annihilated if we emerged in the same space with solid matter. The detector prevents the projector from stopping if it senses such a structure." Saunders grinned savagely. "Some damned idiot must have built a house right where we are!"

The needle passed its limit, and still they droned on through a featureless grayness. Saunders reset the dial and noted the first half millennium. It was nice, though not necessary, to know what year it was when they emerged.

He wasn't worried at first. Man's works were so horribly impermanent; he thought with a sadness of the cities and civilizations he had seen rise and spend their little hour and sink back into the night and chaos of time. But after a thousand years . . .

Two thousand . . .

Three thousand . . .

Belgotai's face was white and tense in the dull glow of the instrument panel. "How long to go?" he whispered.

"I—don't—know."

Within the machine, the long minutes passed while the projector hummed its song of power and two men stared with hypnotized fascination at the creeping record of centuries.

For twenty thousand years that incredible thing stood. In the year 25,296 A.D., the switch suddenly went down under Saunders' steady tug. The machine flashed into reality, tilted, and slid down a few feet before coming to rest. Wildly, they opened the door.

The projector lay on a stone block big as a small house, whose ultimate slipping from its place had freed them. It was halfway up a pyramid.

A monument of gray stone, a tetrahedron a

mile to a side and a half a mile high. The outer casing had worn away, or been removed, so that the tremendous blocks stood naked to the weather. Soil had drifted up onto it, grass and trees grew on its titanic slopes. Their roots, and wind and rain and frost, were slowly crumbling the artificial hill to earth again, but still it dominated the landscape.

A defaced carving leered out from a tangle of brush. Saunders looked at it and looked away, shuddering. No human being had ever carved that thing.

The countryside around was altered; he couldn't see the old river and there was a lake glimmering in the distance which had not been there before. The hills seemed lower, and forest covered them. It was a wild, primeval scene, but there was a spaceship standing near the base, a monster machine with its nose rearing skyward and a sunburst blazon on its hull. And there were men working nearby.

Saunders' shout rang in the still air. He and Belgotai scrambled down the steep slopes of earth, clawing past trees and vines. Men!

No—not all men. A dozen great shining engines were toiling without supervision at the foot of the pyramid—robots. And of the group which turned to stare at the travelers, two were squat, blue-furred, with snouted faces and six-fingered hands.

Saunders realized with an unexpectedly eerie shock that he was seeing extraterrestrial intelligence. But it was to the men that he faced.

They were all tall, with aristocratically refined features and a calm that seemed inbred.

Their clothing was impossible to describe, it was like a rainbow shimmer around them, never the same in its play of color and shape. So, thought Saunders, so must the old gods have looked on high Olympus, beings greater and more beautiful than man.

But it was a human voice that called to them, a deep, well-modulated tone in a totally foreign language. Saunders remembered exasperatedly that he had forgotten the psychophone. But one of the blue-furred aliens was already fetching a round, knob-studded globe out of which the familiar translating voice seemed to come: ". . . time travelers."

"From the very remote past, obviously," said another man. Damn him, damn them all, they weren't any more excited than at the bird which rose, startled, from the long grass. You'd think time travelers would at least be worth shaking by the hand.

"Listen," snapped Saunders, realizing in the back of his mind that his annoyance was a reaction against the awesomeness of the company, "we're in trouble. Our machine won't carry us back, and we have to find a period of time which knows how to reverse the effect. Can you do it?"

One of the aliens shook his animal head. "No," he said. "There is no way known to physics of getting farther back than about seventy years. Beyond that, the required energy approaches infinity and—"

Saunders groaned. "We know it," said Belgotai harshly.

"At least you must rest," said one of the men

in a more kindly tone. "It will be interesting to hear your story."

"I've told it to too many people in the last few millennia," rasped Saunders. "Let's hear yours for a change."

Two of the strangers exchanged low-voiced words. Saunders could almost translate them himself: *Barbarians—childish emotional pattern—well, humor them for a while.*

"This is an archaeological expedition, excavating the pyramid," said one of the men patiently. "We are from the Galactic Institute, Sarlan-sector branch. I am Lord Arsfel of Astracyr, and these are my subordinates. The nonhumans, as you may wish to know, are from the planet Quulhan, whose sun is not visible from Terra."

Despite himself, Saunders' awed gaze turned to the stupendous mass looming over them. "Who built it?" he breathed.

"The Ixchulhi made such structures on planets they conquered, no one knows why. But then, no one knows what they were, or where they came from, or where they ultimately went. It is hoped that some of the answers may be found in their pyramids."

The atmosphere grew more relaxed. Deftly, the men of the expedition got Saunders' and Belgotai's stories and what information about their almost prehistoric periods they cared for. In exchange, something of history was offered them.

After the Ixchulhi's ruinous wars the Galaxy had made a surprisingly rapid comeback. New techniques of mathematical psychology made it possible to unite the peoples of a billion worlds and rule them effectively. The Galactic Empire was egalitarian—it had to be, for one of its mainstays was the fantastically old and evolved race of the planet called Vro-Hi by men.

It was peaceful, prosperous, colorful with diversity of races and cultures, expanding in science and the arts. It had already endured for ten thousand years, and there seemed no doubt in Arsfel's calm mind that it could endure forever. The barbarians along the Galactic periphery and out in the Magellanic Clouds? Nonsense! The Empire would get around to civilizing them in due course; meanwhile they were only a nuisance.

But Sol could almost be called one of the barbarian suns, though it lay within the Imperial boundaries. Civilization was concentrated near the center of the Galaxy, and Sol lay up in what was actually a remote and thinly starred region of space. A few primitive landsmen still lived on its planets and had infrequent intercourse with the nearer stars, but they hardly counted. The human race had almost forgotten its ancient home.

Somehow the picture was saddening to the American. He thought of old Earth spinning on her lonely way through the emptiness of space, he thought of the great arrogant Empire and of all the mighty dominions which had fallen to dust through the millennia. But when he ventured to suggest that this civilization, too, was not immortal, he was immediately snowed under with figures, facts, logic, the curious para-mathematical symbolism of modern mass psychology. It could be shown rigorously that the present setup was inherently stable—and already ten thousand years of history had given no evidence to upset that science. . . .

"I give up," said Saunders. "I can't argue with you."

They were shown through the spaceship's immense interior, the luxurious apartments of the expedition, the looming intricate machinery which did its own thinking. Arsfel tried to show them his art, his recorded music, his psychobooks, but it was no use, they didn't have the understanding.

Savages! Could an Australian aborigine have appreciated Rembrandt, Beethoven, Kant, or Einstein? Could he have lived happily in sophisticated New York society?

"We'd best go," muttered Belgotai. "We don't belong heah."

Saunders nodded. Civilization had gone too far for them, they could never be more than frightened pensioners in its hugeness. Best to get on their way again.

"I would advise you to leap ahead for long intervals," said Arsfel. "Galactic civilization won't have spread out this far for many thousands of years, and certainly whatever native culture Sol develops won't be able to help you." He smiled. "It doesn't matter if you overshoot the time when the process you need is invented. The records won't be lost, I assure you. From here on, you are certain of encountering only peace and enlightenment . . . unless, of course, the barbarians of Terra get hostile, but then you can always leave them behind. Sooner or later, there will be true civilization here to help you."

"Tell me honestly," said Saunders. "Do you think the negative time machine will ever be invented?"

One of the beings from Quulhan shook his strange head. "I doubt it," he said gravely. "We would have had visitors from the future."

"They might not have cared to see your time," argued Saunders desperately. "They'd have complete records of it. So they'd go back to investigate more primitive ages, where their appearance might easily pass unnoticed."

"You may be right," said Arsfel. His tone was disconcertingly like that with which an adult comforts a child by a white lie.

"Le's go!" snarled Belgotai.

In 26,000 the forests still stood and the pyramid had become a high hill where trees nodded and rustled in the wind.

In 27,000 a small village of wood and stone houses stood among smiling grain fields.

In 28,000 men were tearing down the pyramid, quarrying it for stone. But its huge bulk was not gone before 30,000 A.D., and a small city had been built from it.

Minutes ago, thought Saunders grayly, they had been talking to Lord Arsfel of Astracyr, and now he was five thousand years in his grave.

In 31,000 they materialized on one of the broad lawns that reached between the towers of a high and proud city. Aircraft swarmed overhead and a spaceship, small beside Arsfel's but nonetheless impressive, was standing nearby.

"Looks like de Empire's got heah," said Belgotai.

"I don't know," said Saunders. "But it looks peaceful, anyway. Let's go out and talk to people."

They were received by tall, stately women in white robes of classic lines. It seemed that the Matriarchy now ruled Sol, and would they please conduct themselves as befitted the inferior sex? No, the Empire hadn't ever gotten out here; Sol paid tribute, and there was an Imperial legate at Sirius, but the actual boundaries of Galactic culture hadn't changed for the past three millennia. Solar civilization was strictly home-grown and obviously superior to the alien influence of the Vro-Hi.

No, nothing was known about time theory. Their visit had been welcome and all that, but now would they please go on? They didn't fit in with the neatly regulated culture of Terra.

"I don't like it," said Saunders as they walked back toward the machine. "Arsfel swore the Imperium would keep expanding its actual as well as its nominal sphere of influence. But it's gone static now. Why?"

"Ih tink," said Belgotai, "dat spite of all his fancy mathematics, yuh were right. Nawthing lasts forever."

"But—my God!"

CHAPTER IV
End of Empire

34,000 A.D. The Matriarchy was gone. The city was a tumbled heap of fire-blackened rocks. Skeletons lay in the ruins.

"The barbarians are moving again," said Saunders bleakly. "They weren't here so very long ago; these bones are still fresh, and they've got a long ways to go to dead center. An empire like this one will be many thousands of years in dying. But it's doomed already."

"What'll we do?" asked Belgotai.

"Go on," said Saunders tonelessly. "What else can we do?"

35,000 A.D. A peasant hut stood under huge old trees. Here and there a broken column stuck out of the earth, remnant of the city. A bearded man in coarsely woven garments fled wildly with his woman and brood of children as the machine appeared.

36,000 A.D. There was a village again, with a battered old spaceship standing hard by. There were half a dozen different races, including man, moving about, working on the construction of some enigmatic machine. They were dressed in plain, shabby clothes, with guns at their sides and the hard look of warriors in their eyes. But they didn't treat the new arrivals too badly.

Their chief was a young man in the cape and helmet of an officer of the Empire. But his outfit was at least a century old, and he was simply head of a small troop which had been hired from among the barbarian hordes to protect this part of Terra. Oddly, he insisted he was a loyal vassal of the Emperor.

The Empire! It was still a remote glory, out there among the stars. Slowly it waned, slowly the barbarians encroached while corruption and civil war tore it apart from the inside, but it was still the pathetic, futile hope of intelligent beings throughout the Galaxy. Some day it would be restored. Some day civilization would return to the darkness of the outer worlds, greater and more splendid than ever. Men dared not believe otherwise.

"But we've got a job right here," shrugged the chief. "Tautho of Sirius will be on Sol's necks soon. I doubt if we can stand him off for long."

"And what'll yuh do den?" challenged Belgotai.

The young-old face twisted in a bitter smile. "Die, of course. What else is there to do—these days?"

They stayed overnight with the troopers. Belgotai had fun swapping lies about warlike exploits, but in the morning he decided to go on with Saunders. The age was violent enough, but its hopelessness daunted even his tough soul.

Saunders looked haggardly at the control panel. "We've got to go a long ways ahead," he said. "A hell of a long ways."

50,000 A.D. They flashed out of the time drive and opened the door. A raw wind caught at them, driving thin sheets of snow before it. The sky hung low and gray over a landscape of high rocky hills where pine trees stood gloomily between naked crags. There was ice on the river that murmured darkly out of the woods.

Geology didn't work that fast; even fourteen thousand years wasn't a very long time to the slowly changing planets. It must have been the work of intelligent beings, ravaging and scoring the world with senseless wars of unbelievable forces.

A gray stone mass dominated the landscape. It stood enormous a few miles off, its black walls sprawling over incredible acres, its massive crenellated towers reaching gauntly into the sky. And it lay half in ruin, torn and tumbled stone distorted by energies that once made rock run molten, blurred by uncounted millennia of weather—old.

"Dead," Saunders voice was thin under the hooting wind. "All dead."

"No!" Belgotai's slant eyes squinted against the flying snow. "No, Mahtin, Ih tink Ih see a banner flying."

The wind blew bitterly around them, searing them with its chill. "Shall we go on?" asked Saunders dully.

"Best we go find out wha's happened," said Belgotai. "Dey can do no worse dan kill us, and Ih begin to tink dat's not so bad."

Saunders put on all the clothes he could find and took the psychophone in one chilled hand. Belgotai wrapped his cloak tightly about him. They started toward the gray edifice.

The wind blew and blew. Snow hissed around them, covering the tough gray-green vegetation that hugged the stony ground. Summer on Earth, 50,000 A.D.

As they neared the structure, its monster size grew on them. Some of the towers which still stood must be almost half a mile high, thought Saunders dizzily. But it had a grim, barbaric look; no civilized race had ever built such a fortress.

Two small, swift shapes darted into the air from that cliff-like wall. "Aircraft," said Belgotai laconically. The wind ripped the word from his mouth.

They were ovoidal, without external controls or windows, apparently running on the gravitic forces which had long ago been tamed. One of them hovered overhead, covering the travelers, while the other dropped to the ground. As it landed, Saunders saw that it was old and worn and scarred. But there was a faded sunburst on its side. Some memory of the Empire must still be alive.

Two came out of the little vessel and approached the travelers with guns in their hands. One was human, a tall well-built young man with shoulder-length black hair blowing under a tarnished helmet, a patched purple coat streaming from his cuirassed shoulders, a faded leather kilt and buskins. The other. . . .

He was a little shorter than the man, but immensely broad of chest and limb. Four muscled arms grew from the massive shoulders, and a tufted tail lashed against his clawed feet. His head was big, broad-skulled, with a round half-animal face and cat-like whiskers about the fanged mouth and the split-pupiled yellow eyes. He wore no clothes except a leather harness, but soft blue-gray fur covered the whole great body.

The psychophone clattered out the man's hail: "Who comes?"

"Friends," said Saunders. "We wish only shelter and a little information."

"Where are you from?" There was a harsh, peremptory note in the man's voice. His face—straight, thin-boned, the countenance of a highly bred aristocrat—was gaunt with strain. "What do you want? What sort of spaceship is that you've got down there?"

"Easy, Vargor," rumbled the alien's bass. "That's no spaceship, you can see that."

"No," said Saunders. "It's a time projector."

"Time travelers!" Vargor's intense blue eyes widened. "I heard of such things once, but—time travelers!" Suddenly: "When are you from? Can you help us?"

"We're from very long ago," said Saunders pityingly. "And I'm afraid we're alone and helpless."

Vargor's erect carriage sagged a little. He looked away. But the other being stepped forward with an eagerness in him. "How far back?" he asked. "Where are you going?"

"We're going to hell, most likely. But can you get us inside? We're freezing."

"Of course. Come with us. You'll not take it amiss if I send a squad to inspect your machine? We have to be careful, you know."

The four squeezed into the aircraft and it lifted with a groan of ancient engines. Vargor gestured at the fortress ahead and his tone was a little wild. "Welcome to the hold of Bronto-thor! Welcome to the Galactic Empire!"

"The Empire?"

"Aye, this is the Empire, or what's left of it. A haunted fortress on a frozen ghost world, last fragment of the old Imperium and still trying to pretend that the Galaxy is not dying—that it didn't die millennia ago, that there is something left besides wild beasts howling among the ruins." Vargor's throat caught in a dry sob. "Welcome!"

The alien laid a huge hand on the man's shoulder. "Don't get hysterical, Vargor," he reproved gently. "As long as brave beings hope, the Empire is still alive—whatever they say."

He looked over his shoulder at the others. "You really are welcome," he said. "It's a hard and dreary life we lead here. Taury and the Dreamer will both welcome you gladly." He paused. Then, unsurely, "But best you don't say too much about the ancient time, if you've really seen it. We can't bear too sharp a reminder, you know."

The machine slipped down beyond the wall, over a gigantic flagged courtyard to the monster bulk of the—the donjon, Saunders supposed one could call it. It rose up in several tiers, with pathetic little gardens on the terraces, toward a dome of clear plastic.

The walls, he saw, were immensely thick, with weapons mounted on them which he could see clearly through the drifting snow. Behind the donjon stood several long, barracks-like buildings, and a couple of spaceships which must have been held together by pure faith rested

near what looked like an arsenal. There were
guards on duty, helmeted men with energy ri-
fles, their cloaks wrapped tightly against the
wind, and other folk scurried around under the
monstrous walls, men and women and children.

"There's Taury," said the alien, pointing to a
small group clustered on one of the terraces.
"We may as well land right there." His wide
mouth opened in an alarming smile. "And for-
give me for not introducing myself before. I'm
Hunda of Haamigur, general of the Imperial
armies, and this is Vargor Alfri, prince of the
Empire."

"Yuh crazy?" blurted Belgotai. "What Empire?"

Hunda shrugged. "It's a harmless game, isn't
it? At that, you know, we are the Empire—
legally. Taury is a direct descendant of Maurco
the Doomer, last Emperor to be anointed according to the proper forms. Of course, that was
five thousand years ago, and Maurco had only
three systems left then, but the law is clear.
These hundred or more barbarian pretenders,
human and otherwise, haven't the shadow of a
real claim to the title."

The vessel grounded and they stepped out.
The others waited for them to come up. There
were half a dozen old men, their long beards
blowing wildly in the gale, there was a being
with the face of a long-beaked bird and one that
had the shape of a centauroid.

"The court of the Empress Taury," said
Hunda.

"Welcome." The answer was low and gracious.

Saunders and Belgotai stared dumbly at her. She was tall, tall as a man, but under her tunic of silver links and her furred cloak she was such a woman as they had dreamed of without ever knowing in life. Her proudly lifted head had something of Vargor's looks, the same clean-lined, high-cheeked face, but it was the countenance of a woman, from the broad clear brow to the wide, wondrously chiseled mouth and the strong chin. The cold had flushed the lovely pale planes of her cheeks. Her heavy bronze-red hair was braided about her helmet, with one rebellious lock tumbling softly toward the level, dark brows. Her eyes, huge and oblique and gray as northern seas, were serene on them.

Saunders found tongue. "Thank you, your majesty," he said in a firm voice.

"If it please you, I am Martin Saunders of America, some forty-eight thousand years in the past, and my companion is Belgotai, free companion from Syrtis about a thousand years later. We are at your service for what little we may be able to do."

She inclined her stately head, and her sudden smile was warm and human. "It is a rare pleasure," she said. "Come inside, please. And forget the formality. Tonight let us simply be alive."

They sat in what had been a small council chamber. The great hall was too huge and empty, a cavern of darkness and rustling relics of greatness, hollow with too many memories. But the lesser room had been made livable, hung with tapestries and carpeted with skins.

Fluorotubes cast a white light over it, and a fire crackled cheerfully in the hearth. Had it not been for the wind against the windows, they might have forgotten where they were.

"—and you can never go back?" Taury's voice was sober. "You can never get home again?"

"I don't think so," said Saunders. "From our story, it doesn't look that way, does it?"

"No," said Hunda. "You'd better settle down in some time and make the best of matters."

"Why not with us?" asked Vargor eagerly.

"We'd welcome you with all our hearts," said Taury, "but I cannot honestly advise you to stay. These are evil times."

It was a harsh language they spoke, a ringing metallic tongue brought in by the barbarians. But from her throat, Saunders thought, it was utter music.

"We'll at least stay a few days," he said impulsively. "It's barely possible we can do something."

"I doubt that," said Hunda practically. "We've retrogressed, yes. For instance, the principle of the time projector was lost long ago. But still, there's a lot of technology left which was far beyond your own times."

"I know," said Saunders defensively. "But—well, frankly—we haven't fitted in any other time, as well."

"Will there ever be a decent age again?" asked one of the old courtiers bitterly.

The avian from Klakkahar turned his eyes on Saunders. "It wouldn't be cowardice for you to leave a lost cause which you couldn't possibly aid," he said in his thin, accented tones. "When the Anvardi come, I think we will all die."

"What is de tale of de Dreamer?" asked Belgotai. "You've mentioned some such."

It was like a sudden darkness in the room. There was silence, under the whistling wind, and men sat wrapped in their own cheerless thoughts. Finally Taury spoke.

"He is the last of the Vro-Hi, counselors of the Empire. That one still lives—the Dreamer. But there can never really be another Empire, at least not on the pattern of the old one. No other race is intelligent enough to coordinate it."

Hunda shook his big head, puzzled. "The Dreamer once told me that might be for the best," he said. "But he wouldn't explain."

"How did you happen to come here—to Earth, of all planets?" Saunders asked.

Taury smiled with a certain grim humor. "The last few generations have been one of the Imperium's less fortunate periods," she said. "In short, the most the Emperor ever commanded was a small fleet. My father had even that shot away from him. He fled with three ships, out toward the Periphery. It occurred to him that Sol was worth trying as a refuge."

The Solar System had been cruelly scarred in the dark ages. The great engineering works which had made the other planets habitable were ruined, and Earth herself had been laid waste. There had been a weapon used which consumed atmospheric carbon dioxide. Saunders, remembering the explanation for the Ice Ages offered by geologists of his own time, nodded in dark understanding. Only a few starveling savages lived on the planet now, and indeed the whole Sirius Sector was so desolated that no conqueror thought it worth bothering with.

It had pleased the Emperor to make his race's ancient home the capital of the Galaxy. He had moved into the ruined fortress of Brontothor, built some seven thousand years ago by the nonhuman Grimmani and blasted out of action a millennium later. Renovation of parts of it, installation of weapons and defensive works, institution of agriculture. . . . "Why, he had suddenly acquired a whole planetary system!" said Taury with a half-sad little smile.

She took them down into the underground levels the next day to see the Dreamer. Vargor went along too, walking close beside her, but Hunda stayed topside; he was busy supervising the construction of additional energy screen generators.

They went through immense vaulted caverns hewed out of the rock, dank tunnels of silence where their footfalls echoed weirdly and shadows flitted beyond the dull glow of fluorospheres. Now and then they passed a looming monstrous bulk, the corroded hulk of some old machine. The night and loneliness weighed heavily on them, they huddled together and did not speak for fear of rousing the jeering echoes.

"There were slideways here once," remarked Taury as they started, "but we haven't gotten around to installing new ones. There's too much else to do."

Too much else—a civilization to rebuild, with

*these few broken remnants. How can they dare
even to keep trying in the face of the angry gods?
What sort of courage is it they have?*

Taury walked ahead with the long, swinging
stride of a warrior, a red lioness of a woman in
the wavering shadows. Her gray eyes caught the
light with a supernatural brilliance. Vargor
kept pace, but he lacked her steadiness, his gaze
shifted nervously from side to side as they
moved down the haunted, booming length of the
tunnels. Belgotai went cat-footed, his own restless eyes had merely the habitual wariness of
his hard and desperate lifetime. Again Saunders thought, what a strange company they
were, four humans from the dawn and the dusk
of human civilization, thrown together at the
world's end and walking to greet the last of the
gods. His past life, Eve, MacPherson, the world
of his time, were dimming in his mind, they
were too remote from his present reality. It
seemed as if he had never been anything but a
follower of the Galactic Empress.

They came at last to a door. Taury knocked
softly and swung it open—yes, they were even
back to manual doors now.

Saunders had been prepared for almost anything, but nonetheless the appearance of the
Dreamer was a shock. He had imagined a grave
white-bearded man, or a huge-skulled spider-
thing, or a naked brain pulsing in a machine-
tended case. But the last of the Vro-Hi was—a
monster.

No—not exactly. Not when you discarded human standards, then he even had a weird beauty
of his own. The gross bulk of him sheened with

iridescence, and his many seven-fingered hands were supple and graceful, and the eyes—the eyes were huge pools of molten gold, lambent and wise, a stare too brilliant to meet directly.

He stood up on his stumpy legs as they entered, barely four feet high though the head-body unit was broad and massive. His hooked beak did not open, and the psychophone remained silent, but as the long delicate feelers pointed toward him Saunders thought he heard words, a deep organ voice rolling soundless through the still air: "Greeting, your majesty. Greeting, your highness. Greeting, men out of time, and welcome!"

Telepathy—direct telepathy—so that was how it felt!

"Thank you ... sir." Somehow, the thing rated the title, rated an awed respect to match his own grave formality. "But I thought you were in a trance of concentration till now. How did you know—" Saunders' voice trailed off and he flushed with sudden distaste.

"No, traveler, I did not read your mind as you think. The Vro-Hi always respected privacy and did not read any thoughts save those contained in speech addressed solely to them. But my induction was obvious."

"What were you thinking about in the last trance?" asked Vargor. His voice was sharp with strain. "Did you reach any plan?"

"No, your highness," vibrated the Dreamer. "As long as the factors involved remain constant, we cannot logically do otherwise than we are doing. When new data appear, I will reconsider immediate necessities. No, I was working

211

further on the philosophical basis which the Second Empire must have."

"What Second Empire?" sneered Vargor bitterly.

"The one which will come—some day," answered Taury quietly.

The Dreamer's wise eyes rested on Saunders and Belgotai. "With your permission," he thought, "I would like to scan your complete memory patterns, conscious, subconscious, and cellular. We know so little of your age." As they hesitated: "I assure you, sirs, that a nonhuman being half a million years old can keep secrets, and certainly does not pass moral judgments. And the scanning will be necessary anyway if I am to teach you the present language."

Saunders braced himself. "Go ahead," he said distastefully.

For a moment he felt dizzy, a haze passed over his eyes and there was an eerie thrill along every nerve of him. Taury laid an arm about his waist, bracing him.

It passed. Saunders shook his head, puzzled. "Is that *all*?"

"Aye, sir. A Vro-Hi brain can scan an indefinite number of units simultaneously." With a faint hint of a chuckle: "But did you notice what tongue you just spoke in?"

"I—eh—huh?" Saunders looked wildly at Taury's smiling face. The hard, open-voweled syllables barked from his mouth: "I—by the gods—I can speak Stellarian now!"

"Aye," thought the Dreamer. "The language centers are peculiarly receptive, it is easy to impress a pattern on them. The method of instruction will not work so well for information involving other faculties, but you must admit it is a convenient and efficient way to learn speech."

"Blast off wit me, den," said Belgotai cheerfully. "Ih allays was a dumkoff at languages."

When the Dreamer was through, he thought: "You will not take it amiss if I tell all that what I saw in both your minds was good—brave and honest, under the little neuroses which all beings at your level of evolution cannot help accumulating. I will be pleased to remove those for you, if you wish."

"No, thanks," said Belgotai. "I like my little neuroses."

"I see that you are debating staying here," went on the Dreamer. "You will be valuable, but you should be fully warned of the desperate position we actually are in. This is not a pleasant age in which to live."

"From what I've seen," answered Saunders slowly, "golden ages are only superficially better. They may be easier on the surface, but there's death in them. To travel hopefully, believe me, is better than to arrive."

"That has been true in all past ages, aye. It was the great mistake of the Vro-Hi. We should have know better, with ten million years of civilization behind us." There was a deep and tragic note in the rolling thought-pulse. "But we thought that since we had achieved a static physical state in which the new frontiers and challenges lay within our own minds, all beings at all levels of evolution could and should have developed in them the same ideal.

213

"With our help, and with the use of scientific psychodynamics and the great cybernetic engines, the coordination of a billion planets became possible. It was perfection, in a way—but perfection is death to imperfect beings, and even the Vro-Hi had many shortcomings. I cannot explain all the philosophy to you; it involves concepts you could not fully grasp, but you have seen the workings of the great laws in the rise and fall of cultures. I have proved rigorously that permanence is a self-contradictory concept. There can be no goal to reach, not ever."

"Then the Second Empire will have no better hope than decay and chaos again?" Saunders grinned humorlessly. "Why the devil do you want one?"

Vargor's harsh laugh shattered the brooding silence. "What indeed does it matter?" he cried. "What use to plan the future of the universe, when we are outlaws on a forgotten planet? The Anvardi are coming!" He sobered, and there was a set to his jaw which Saunders liked. "They're coming, and there's little we can do to stop it," said Vargor. "But we'll give them a fight. We'll give them such a fight as the poor old Galaxy never saw before!"

CHAPTER V
Attack of the Anvardi

"Oh, no—oh no—oh no."

The murmur came unnoticed from Vargor's lips, a broken cry of pain as he stared at the image which flickered and wavered on the great interstellar communiscreen. And there was horror in the eyes of Taury, grimness to the set of Hunda's mighty jaws, a sadness of many hopeless centuries in the golden gaze of the Dreamer.

After weeks of preparation and waiting, Saunders realized matters were at last coming to a head.

"Aye, your majesty," said the man in the screen. He was haggard, exhausted, worn out by strain and struggle and defeat. "Aye, fiftyfour shiploads of us, and the Anvardian fleet in pursuit."

"How far behind?" rapped Hunda.

"About half a light-year, sir, and coming up slowly. We'll be close to Sol before they can overhaul us."

"Can you fight them?" rapped Hunda.

"No, sir," said the man. "We're loaded with refugees, women and children and unarmed peasants, hardly a gun on a ship—Can't you help us?" It was a cry, torn by the ripping static that filled the interstellar void. "Can't you help us, your majesty? They'll sell us for slaves!"

"How did it happen?" asked Taury wearily.

"I don't know, your majesty. We heard you were at Sol through your agents, and secretly

gathered ships. We don't want to be under the
Anvardi, Empress; they tax the life from us and
conscript our men and take our women and
children. . . . We only communicated by ultrawave; it can't be traced, and we only used the
code your agents gave us. But as we passed Canopus, they called on us to surrender in the
name of their king—and they have a whole war
fleet after us!"

"How long before they get here?" asked
Hunda.

"At this rate, sir, perhaps a week," answered
the captain of the ship. Static snarled through
his words.

"Well, keep on coming this way," said Taury
wearily. "We'll send ships against them. You
may get away during the battle. Don't go to Sol,
of course, we'll have to evacuate that. Our men
will try to contact you later."

"We aren't worth it, your majesty. Save all
your ships."

"We're coming," said Taury flatly, and broke
the circuit.

She turned to the others, and her red head
was still lifted. "Most of our people can get
away," she said. "They can flee into the Arlath
cluster; the enemy won't be able to find them in
that wilderness." She smiled, a tired little smile
that tugged at one corner of her mouth. "We all
know what to do, we've planned against this
day. Munidor, Falz, Mico, start readying for
evacuation. Hunda, you and I will have to plan
our assault. We'll want to make it as effective
as possible, but use a minimum of ships."

"Why sacrifice fighting strength uselessly?" asked Belgotai.

"It won't be useless. We'll delay the Anvardi, and give those refugees a chance to escape."

"If we had weapons," rumbled Hunda. His huge fists clenched. "By the gods, if we had decent weapons!"

The Dreamer stiffened. And before he could vibrate it, the same thought had leaped into Saunders' brain, and they stared at each other, man and Vro-Hian, with a sudden wild hope. . . .

Space glittered and flared with a million stars, thronging against the tremendous dark, the Milky Way foamed around the sky in a rush of cold silver, and it was shattering to a human in its utter immensity. Saunders felt the loneliness of it as he had never felt it on the trip to Venus—for Sol was dwindling behind them, they were rushing out into the void between the stars.

There had only been time to install the new weapon on the dreadnought, time and facilities were so cruelly short, there had been no chance even to test it in maneuvers. They might, perhaps, have leaped back into time again and again, gaining weeks, but the shops of Terra could only turn out so much material in the one week they did have.

So it was necessary to risk the whole fleet and the entire fighting strength of Sol on this one desperate gamble. If the old *Vengeance* could do her part, the outnumbered Imperials would have their chance. But if they failed . . .

Saunders stood on the bridge, looking out at

the stellar host, trying to discern the Anvardian fleet. The detectors were far over scale, the enemy was close, but you couldn't visually detect something that outran its own image.

Hunda was at the control central, bent over the cracked old dials and spinning the corroded signal wheels, trying to coax another centimeter per second from a ship more ancient than the Pyramids had been in Saunders' day. The Dreamer stood quietly in a corner, staring raptly out at the Galaxy. The others at the court were each in charge of a squadron, Saunders had talked to them over the inter-ship visiscreen—Vargor white-lipped and tense, Belgotai blasphemously cheerful, the rest showing only cool reserve.

"In a few minutes," said Taury quietly. "In just a few minutes, Martin."

She paced back from the viewport, lithe and restless as a tigress. The cold white starlight glittered in her eyes. A red cloak swirled about the strong, deep curves of her body, a Sunburst helmet sat proudly on her bronze-bright hair. Saunders thought how beautiful she was—by all the gods, how beautiful!

She smiled at him. "It is your doing, Martin," she said. "You came from the past just to bring us hope. It's enough to make one believe in destiny." She took his hand. "But of course it's not the hope you wanted. This won't get you back home."

"It doesn't matter," he said.

"It does, Martin. But—may I say it? I'm still glad of it. Not only for the sake of the Empire, but—"

A voice rattled over the bridge communicator: "Ultrawave to bridge. The enemy is sending us a message, your majesty. Shall I send it up to you?"

"Of course." Taury switched on the bridge screen.

A face leaped into it, strong and proud and ruthless, the Sunburst shining in the green hair. "Greeting, Taury of Sol," said the Anvardian. "I am Ruulthan, Emperor of the Galaxy."

"I know who you are," said Taury thinly, "but I don't recognize your assumed title."

"Our detectors report your approach with a fleet approximately one-tenth the size of ours. You have one Supernova ship, of course, but so do we. Unless you wish to come to terms, it will mean annihilation."

"What are your terms?"

"Surrender, execution of the criminals who led the attacks on Anvardian planets, and your own pledge of allegiance to me as Galactic Emperor." The voice was clipped, steel-hard.

Taury turned away in disgust. Saunders told Ruulthan in explicit language what to do with his terms, and then cut off the screen.

Taury gestured to the newly installed time-drive controls. "Take them, Martin," she said. "They're yours, really." She put her hands in his and looked at him with serious gray eyes. "And if we should fail in this—good-bye, Martin."

"Good-bye," he said thickly.

He wrenched himself over the panel and sat down before its few dials. *Here goes nothing!*

He waved one hand, and Hunda cut off the hyperdrive. At low intrinsic velocity, the *Vengeance* hung in space while the invisible ships of her fleet flashed past toward the oncoming Anvardi.

Slowly then, Saunders brought down the time-drive switch. And the ship roared with power, atomic energy flowed into the mighty circuits which they had built to carry her huge mass through time—the lights dimmed, the giant machine throbbed and pulsed, and a featureless grayness swirled beyond the ports.

He took her back three days. They lay in empty space, the Anvardi were still fantastic distances away. His eyes strayed to the brilliant yellow spark of Sol. Right there, this minute, he was sweating his heart out installing the time projector which had just carried him back. . . .

But no, that was meaningless, simultaneity was arbitrary. And there was a job to do right now.

The chief astrogator's voice came with a torrent of figures. They had to find the exact position in which the Anvardian flagship would be in precisely seventy-two hours. Hunda rang the signals to the robots in the engine room, and slowly, ponderously, the *Vengeance* slid across five million miles of space.

"All set," said Hunda. "Let's go!"

Saunders smiled, a mirthless skinning of teeth, and threw his main switch in reverse. Three days forward in time. . . .

To lie alongside the Anvardian dreadnought!

Frantically Hunda threw the hyperdrive back in, matching translight velocities. They could see the ship now, it loomed like a metal mountain against the stars. And every gun in the *Vengeance* cut loose!

Vortex cannon—blasters—atomic shells and torpedoes—gravity snatchers—all the hell which had ever been brewed in the tortured centuries of history vomited against the screens of the Anvardian flagship.

Under that monstrous barrage, filling space with raving energy till it seemed its very structure must boil, the screens went down, a flare of light searing like another nova. And through the solid matter of her hull those weapons bored, cutting, blasting, disintegrating. Steel boiled into vapor, into atoms, into pure devouring energy that turned on the remaining solid material. Through and through the hull that fury raged, a waste of flame that left not even ash in its track.

And now the rest of the Imperial fleet drove against the Anvardi. Assaulted from outside, with a devouring monster in its very midst, the Anvardian fleet lost the offensive, recoiled and broke up into desperately fighting units. War snarled between the silent white stars.

Still the Anvardi fought, hurling themselves against the ranks of the Imperials, wrecking ships and slaughtering men even as they went down. They still had the numbers, if not the organization, and they had the same weapons and the same bitter courage of their foes.

The bridge of the *Vengeance* shook and roared with the shock of battle. The lights darkened, flickered back, dimmed again. The riven air was sharp with ozone, and the intolerable energies loosed made her interior a furnace. Reports clattered over the communicator: "—Number Three screen down—Compartment Number Five doesn't answer—Vortex turret Five Hundred Thirty Seven out of action—"

Still she fought, still she fought, hurling metal and energy in an unending storm, raging and rampaging among the ships of the Anvardi. Saunders found himself manning a gun, shooting out at vessels he couldn't see, getting his aim by sweat-blinded glances at the instruments—and the hours dragged away in flame and smoke and racking thunder. . . ."

"They're fleeing!"

The exuberant shout rang through every remaining compartment of the huge old ship. *Victory, victory, victory*—she had not heard such cheering for five thousand weary years.

Saunders staggered drunkenly back onto the bridge. He could see the scattered units of the Anvardi now that he was behind them, exploding out into the Galaxy in wild search of refuge, hounded and harried by the vengeful Imperial fleet.

And now the Dreamer stood up, and suddenly he was not a stump-legged little monster but a living god whose awful thought leaped across space, faster than light, to bound and roar through the skulls of the barbarians. Saunders fell to the floor under the impact of that mighty shout, he lay numbly staring at the impassive stars while the great command rang in his shuddering brain:

"Soldiers of the Anvardi, your false emperor is dead and Taury the Red, Empress of the Gal-

axy, has the victory. You have seen her power. Do not resist it longer, for it is unstoppable.

"Lay down your arms. Surrender to the mercy of the Imperium. We pledge you amnesty and safe-conduct. And bear this word back to your planets:

"Taury the Red calls on all the chiefs of the Anvardian Confederacy to pledge fealty to her and aid her in restoring the Galactic Empire!"

CHAPTER VI
Flight Without End

They stood on a balcony of Brontothor and looked again at old Earth for the first time in almost a year and the last time, perhaps, in their lives.

It was strange to Saunders, this standing again on the planet which had borne him after those months in the many and alien worlds of a Galaxy huger than he could really imagine. There was an odd little tug at his heart, for all the bright hope of the future. He was saying good-bye to Eve's world.

But Eve was gone, she was part of a past forty-eight thousand years dead, and he had *seen* those years rise and die, his one year of personal time was filled and stretched by the vision of history until Eve was a remote, lovely dream. God keep her, wherever her soul had wandered in these millennia—God grant she had had a happy life—but as for him, he had his own life to live, and a mightier task at hand than he had ever conceived.

The last months rose in his mind, a bewilderment of memory. After the surrender of the Anvardian fleet, the Imperials had gone under their escort directly to Canopus and thence through the Anvardian empire. And chief after chief, now that Ruulthan was dead and Taury had shown she could win a greater mastery than his, pledged allegiance to her.

Hunda was still out there with Belgotai, fighting a stubborn Anvardian earl. The Dreamer was in the great Polarian System, toiling at readjustment. It would be necessary, of course, for the Imperial capital to move from isolated Sol to central Polaris, and Taury did not think she would ever have time or opportunity to visit Earth again.

And so she had crossed a thousand starry light-years to the little lonely sun which had been her home. She brought ships, machines, troops. Sol would have a military base sufficient to protect it. Climate engineers would drive the glacial winter of Earth back to its poles and begin the resettlement of the other planets. There would be schools, factories, civilization, Sol would have cause to remember its Empress.

Saunders came along because he couldn't quite endure the thought of leaving Earth altogether without farewell. Vargor, grown ever more silent and moody, joined them, but otherwise the old comradeship of Brontothor was dissolving in the sudden fury of work and war and complexity which claimed them.

And so they stood again in the old ruined castle, Saunders and Taury, looking out at the night of Earth.

It was late, all others seemed to be asleep. Below the balcony, the black walls drooped dizzily to the gulf of night that was the main courtyard. Beyond it, a broken section of outer wall showed snow lying white and mystic under the moon. The stars were huge and frosty, flashing and glittering with cold crystal light above the looming pines, grandeur and arrogance and remoteness wheeling enormously across the silent sky. The moon rode high, its scarred old face the only familiarity from Saunders' age, its argent radiance flooding down on the snow to shatter in a million splinters.

It was quiet, sound seemed to have frozen to death in the bitter windless cold. Saunders had stood alone, wrapped in furs with his breath shining ghostly from his nostrils, looking out on the silent winter world and thinking his own thoughts. He had heard a soft footfall and turned to see Taury approaching.

"I couldn't sleep," she said.

She came out onto the balcony to stand beside him. The moonlight was white on her face, shimmering faintly from her eyes and hair, she seemed a dim goddess of the night.

"What were you thinking, Martin?" she asked after a while.

"Oh—I don't know," he said. "Just dreaming a little, I suppose. It's a strange thought to me, to have left my own time forever and now to be leaving even my own world."

She nodded gravely. "I know. I feel the same way." Her low voice dropped to a whisper. "I didn't have to come back in person, you know. They need me more at Polaris. But I thought I deserved this last farewell to the days when we fought with our own hands, and fared between the stars, when we were a small band of sworn comrades whose dreams outstripped our strength. It was hard and bitter, yes, but I don't think we'll have time for laughter anymore. When you work for a million stars, you don't have a chance to see one peasant's wrinkled face light with a deed of kindness you did, or hear him tell you what you did wrong—the world will all be strangers to us—"

For another moment, silence under the far cold stars, then, "Martin—I am so lonely now."

He took her in his arms. Her lips were cold against his, cold with the cruel silent chill of the night, but she answered him with a fierce yearning.

"I think I love you, Martin," she said after a very long time. Suddenly she laughed, a clear and lovely music echoing from the frosty towers of Brontothor. "Oh, Martin, I shouldn't have been afraid. We'll never be lonely, not ever again—"

The moon had sunk far toward the dark horizon when he took her back to her rooms. He kissed her good night and went down the booming corridor toward his own chambers.

His head was awhirl—he was drunk with the sweetness and wonder of it, he felt like singing and laughing aloud and embracing the whole starry universe. Taury, Taury, Taury!

"Martin."

He paused. There was a figure standing before his door, a tall slender form wrapped in a dark cloak. The dull light of a fluoroglobe threw the face into sliding shadow and tormented highlights. Vargor.

"What is it?" he asked.

The prince's hand came up, and Saunders saw the blunt muzzle of a stun pistol gaping at him. Vargor smiled, lopsidedly and sorrowfully, "I'm sorry, Martin," he said.

Saunders stood paralyzed with unbelief. Vargor—why, Vargor had fought beside him; they'd saved each other's lives, laughed and worked and lived together—Vargor!

The gun flashed. There was a crashing in Saunders' head and he tumbled into illimitable darkness.

He awoke very slowly, every nerve tingling with the pain of returning sensation. Something was restraining him. As his vision cleared, he saw that he was lying bound and gagged on the floor of his time projector.

The time machine—he'd all but forgotten it, left it standing in a shed while he went out to the stars; he'd never thought to have another look at it. The time machine!

Vargor stood in the open door, a fluoroglobe in one hand lighting his haggard face. His hair fell in disarray past his tired, handsome features, and his eyes were as wild as the low words that spilled from his mouth.

227

"I'm sorry, Martin, really I am. I like you, and you've done the Empire such a service as it can never forget, and this is as low a trick as one man can ever play on another. But I have to. I'll be haunted by the thought of this night all my life, but I have to."

Saunders tried to move, snarling incoherently through his gag. Vargor shook his head. "Oh, no, Martin, I can't risk letting you make an outcry. If I'm to do evil, I'll at least do a competent job of it.

"I love Taury, you see. I've loved her ever since I first met her, when I came from the stars with a fighting fleet to her father's court and saw her standing there with the frost crackling through her hair and those gray eyes shining at me. I love her so it's like a pain in me. I can't be away from her, I'd pull down the cosmos for her sake. And I thought she was slowly coming to love me.

"And tonight I saw you two on the balcony, and knew I'd lost. Only I can't give up! Our breed has fought the Galaxy for a dream, Martin—it's not in us ever to stop fighting while life is in us. Fighting by any means, for whatever is dear and precious—but fighting!"

Vargor made a gesture of deprecation. "I don't want power, Martin, believe me. The consort's job will be hard and unglamorous, galling to a man of spirit—but if that's the only way to have her, then so be it. And I do honestly believe, right or wrong, that I'm better for her and for the Empire than you. You don't really belong here, you know. You don't have the tradition, the feeling, the training—you don't even have the biological heritage of five thousand years. Taury may care for you now, but think twenty years ahead!"

Vargor smiled wryly. "I'm taking a chance, of course. If you do find a means of negative time travel and come back here, it will be disgrace and exile for me. It would be safer to kill you. But I'm not quite that much of a scoundrel. I'm giving you your chance. At worst, you should escape into the time when the Second Empire is in its glorious bloom, a happier age than this. And if you do find a means to come back—well, remember what I said about your not belonging, and try to reason with clarity and kindness. Kindness to Taury, Martin."

He lifted the fluoroglobe, casting its light over the dim interior of the machine. "So it's good-bye, Martin, and I hope you won't hate me too much. It should take you several thousand years to work free and stop the machine. I've equipped it with weapons, supplies, everything I think you may need for any eventuality. But I'm sure you'll emerge in a greater and more peaceful culture, and be happier there."

His voice was strangely tender, all of a sudden. "Good-bye, Martin my comrade. And—good luck!"

He opened the main-drive switch and stepped out as the projector began to warm up. The door clanged shut behind him.

Saunders writhed on the floor, cursing with a brain that was a black cauldron of bitterness. The great drone of the projector rose, he was on his way—*Oh no—stop the machine, God, set me free before it's too late!*

The plastic cords cut his wrists. He was lashed to a stanchion, unable to reach the switch with any part of his body. His groping fingers slid across the surface of a knot, the nails clawing for a hold. The machine roared with full power, driving ahead through the vastness of time.

Vargor had bound him skillfully. It took him a long time to get free. Toward the end he went slowly, not caring, knowing with a dull knowledge that he was already more thousands of irretrievable years into the future than his dials would register.

He climbed to his feet, plucked the gag from his mouth, and looked blankly out at the faceless gray. The century needle was hard against its stop. He estimated vaguely that he was some ten thousand years into the future already.

Ten thousand years!

He yanked down the switch with a raging burst of savagery.

It was dark outside. He stood stupidly for a moment before he saw water seeping into the cabin around the door. Water—he was under water—short circuits! Frantically, he slammed the switch forward again.

He tasted the water on the floor. It was salt. Sometime in that ten thousand years, for reasons natural or artificial, the sea had come in and covered the site of Brontothor.

A thousand years later he was still below its surface. Two thousand, three thousand, ten thousand. . . .

Taury, Taury! For twenty thousand years she had been dust on an alien planet. And Belgotai

230

was gone with his wry smile, Hunda's staunchness, even the Dreamer must long ago have descended into darkness. The sea rolled over dead Brontothor, and he was alone.

He bowed his head on his arms and wept.

For three million years the ocean lay over Brontothor's land. And Saunders drove onward.

He stopped at intervals to see if the waters had gone. Each time the frame of the machine groaned with pressure and the sea poured in through the crack of the door. Otherwise he sat dully in the throbbing loneliness, estimating time covered by his own watch and the known rate of the projector, not caring anymore about dates or places.

Several times he considered stopping the machine, letting the sea burst in and drown him. There would be peace in its depths, sleep and forgetting. But no, it wasn't in him to quit that easily. Death was his friend, death would always be there waiting for his call.

But Taury was dead.

Time grayed to its end. In the four millionth year, he stopped the machine and discovered that there was dry air around him.

He was in a city. But it was not such a city as he had ever seen or imagined, he couldn't follow the wild geometry of the titanic structures that loomed about him and they were never the same. The place throbbed and pulsed with incredible forces, it wavered and blurred in a strangely unreal light. Great devastating energies flashed and roared around him—lightning come to Earth. The air hissed and stung with their booming passage.

The thought was a shout filling his skull, blazing along his nerves, too mighty a thought for his stunned brain to do more than grope after meaning:

CREATURE FROM OUT OF TIME, LEAVE THIS PLACE AT ONCE OR THE FORCES WE USE WILL DESTROY YOU!

Through and through him that mental vision seared, down to the very molecules of his brain, his life lay open to Them in a white flame of incandescence.

Can you help me? he cried to the gods. *Can you send me back through time?*

MAN, THERE IS NO WAY TO TRAVEL FAR BACKWARD IN TIME, IT IS INHERENTLY IMPOSSIBLE. YOU MUST GO ON TO THE VERY END OF THE UNIVERSE, AND BEYOND THE END, BECAUSE THAT WAY LIES—

He screamed with the pain of unendurably great thought and concept filling his human brain.

GO ON, MAN, GO ON! BUT YOU CANNOT SURVIVE IN THAT MACHINE AS IT IS. I WILL CHANGE IT FOR YOU . . . GO!

The time projector started again by itself. Saunders fell forward into a darkness that roared and flashed.

Grimly, desperately, like a man driven by demons, Saunders hurtled into the future.

There could be no gainsaying the awful word which had been laid on him. The mere thought of the gods had engraved itself on the very tissue of his brain. Why he should go on to the end of time, he could not imagine, nor did he care. But go on he must!

The machine had been altered. It was airtight now, and experiment showed the window to be utterly unbreakable. Something had been done to the projector so that it hurled him forward at an incredible rate, millions of years passed while a minute or two ticked away within the droning shell.

But what had the gods been?

He would never know. Beings from beyond the Galaxy, beyond the very universe—the ultimately evolved descendants of man—something at whose nature he could not even guess—there was no way of telling. This much was plain: whether it had become extinct or had changed into something else, the human race was gone. Earth would never feel human tread again.

I wonder what became of the Second Empire? I hope it had a long and good life. Or—could that have been its unimaginable end product?

The years reeled past, millions, billions mounting on each other while Earth spun around her star and the Galaxy aged. Saunders fled onward.

He stopped now and then, unable to resist a glimpse of the world and its tremendous history.

A hundred million years in the future, he looked out on great sheets of flying snow. The gods were gone. Had they too died, or abandoned Earth—perhaps for an altogether different plane of existence? He would never know.

There was a being coming through the storm. The wind flung the snow about him in whirling, hissing clouds. Frost was in his gray fur. He moved with a lithe, unhuman grace, carrying a curved staff at whose tip was a blaze like a tiny sun.

Saunders hailed him through the psychophone, letting his amplified voice shout through the blizzard: "Who are you? What are you doing on Earth?"

The being carried a stone ax in one hand and wore a string of crude beads about his neck. But he stared with bold yellow eyes at the machine and the psychophone brought his harsh scream: "You must be from the far past, one of the earlier cycles."

"They told me to go on, back almost a hundred million years ago. They told me to go to the end of time!"

The psychophone hooted with metallic laughter. "If *They* told you so—then go!"

The being walked on into the storm.

Saunders flung himself ahead. There was no place on Earth for him anymore, he had no choice but to go on.

A billion years in the future there was a city standing on a plain where grass grew that was blue and glassy and tinkled with a high crystalline chiming as the wind blew through it. But the city had never been built by humans, and it warned him away with a voice he could not disobey.

Then the sea came, and for a long time thereafter he was trapped within a mountain; he had to drive onward till it had eroded back to the ground.

The sun grew hotter and whiter as the hydrogen-helium cycle increased its intensity. Earth spiraled slowly closer to it, the friction of gas and dust clouds in space taking their infinitesimal toll of its energy over billions of years.

How many intelligent races had risen on Earth and had their day, and died, since the age when man first came out of the jungle? *At least,* he thought tiredly, *we were the first.*

A hundred billion years in the future, the sun had used up its last reserves of nuclear reactions. Saunders looked out on a bare mountain scene, grim as the Moon—but the Moon had long ago fallen back toward its parent world and exploded into a meteoric rain. Earth faced its primary now; its day was as long as its year. Saunders saw part of the sun's huge blood-red disc shining wanly.

So good-bye, Sol, he thought. *Good-bye, and thank you for many million years of warmth and light. Sleep well, old friend.*

Some billions of years beyond, there was nothing but the elemental dark. Entropy had reached a maximum, the energy sources were used up, the universe was dead.

The universe was dead!

He screamed with the graveyard terror of it and flung the machine onward. Had it not been for the gods' command, he might have let it hang there, might have opened the door to airlessness and absolute zero to die. But he had to go on. He had reached the end of all things, but he had to go on. *Beyond the end of time—*

Billions upon billions of years fled. Saunders lay in his machine, sunk into an apathetic coma. Once he roused himself to eat, feeling the sardonic humor of the situation—the last living creature, the last free energy in all the cindered cosmos, fixing a sandwich.

Many billions of years in the future, Saunders paused again. He looked out into blackness. But with a sudden shock he discerned a far faint glow, the vaguest imaginable blur of light out in the heavens.

Trembling, he jumped forward another billion years. The light was stronger now, a great sprawling radiance swirling inchoately in the sky.

The universe was re-forming.

It made sense, thought Saunders, fighting for self-control. Space had expanded to some kind of limit, now it was collapsing in on itself to start the cycle anew—the cycle that had been repeated none knew how many times in the past. The universe was mortal, but it was a phoenix which would never really die.

But he was disturbingly mortal, and suddenly he was free of his death wish. At the very least he wanted to see what the next time around looked like. But the universe would, according to the best theories of twentieth-century cosmology, collapse to what was virtually a point-source, a featureless blaze of pure energy out of which the primal atoms would be reformed. If he wasn't to be devoured in that raging furnace, he'd better leap a long ways ahead. A hell of a long ways!

He grinned with sudden reckless determination and plunged the switch forward.

Worry came back. How did he know that a planet would be formed under him? He might come out in open space, or in the heart of a sun . . . Well, he'd have to risk that. The gods must have foreseen and allowed for it.

He came out briefly—and flashed back into time-drive. The planet was still molten!

Some geological ages later, he looked out at a spuming gray rain, washing with senseless power from a hidden sky, covering naked rocks with a raging swirl of white water. He didn't go out; the atmosphere would be unbreathable until plants had liberated enough oxygen.

On and on! Sometimes he was under seas, sometimes on land. He saw strange jungles like overgrown ferns and mosses rise and wither in the cold of a glacial age and rise again in altered life-form.

A thought nagged at him, tugging at the back of his mind as he rode onward. It didn't hit him for several million years, then: *The moon! Oh, my God, the moon!*

His hands trembled too violently for him to stop the machine. Finally, with an effort, he controlled himself enough to pull the switch. He skipped on, looking for a night of full moon.

Luna. The same old face—*Luna*!

The shock was too great to register. Numbly, he resumed his journey. And the world began to look familiar, there were low forested hills and a river shining in the distance . . .

He didn't really believe it till he saw the village. It was the same—Hudson, New York.

He sat for a moment, letting his physicist's brain consider the tremendous fact. In Newtonian terms, it meant that every particle newly formed in the Beginning had exactly the same position and velocity as every corresponding particle formed in the previous cycle. In more acceptable Einsteinian language, the continuum was spherical in all four dimensions. In any case—if you traveled long enough, through space of time, you got back to your starting point.

He could go home!

He ran down the sunlit hill, heedless of his foreign garments, ran till the breath sobbed in raw lungs and his heart seemed about to burst from the ribs. Gasping, he entered the village, went into a bank, and looked at the tear-off calendar and the wall clock.

June, 17, 1936, 1:30 P.M. From that, he could figure his time of arrival in 1973 to the minute.

He walked slowly back, his legs trembling under him, and started the time machine again. Grayness was outside—for the last time.

1973.

Martin Saunders stepped out of the machine. Its moving in space, at Brontothor, had brought it outside MacPherson's house; it lay halfway up the hill at the top of which the rambling old building stood.

There came a flare of soundless energy. Saunders sprang back in alarm and saw the machine dissolve into molten metal—into gas—into a nothingness that shone briefly and was gone.

The gods must have put some annihilating device into it. They didn't want its devices from the future loose in the twentieth century.

But there was no danger of that, thought Saunders as he walked slowly up the hill through the rain-wet grass. He had seen too much of war and horror ever to give men knowledge they weren't ready for. He and Eve and MacPherson would have to suppress the story of his return around time—for that would offer a means of travel into the past, remove the barrier which would keep man from too much use of the machine for murder and oppression. The Second Empire and the Dreamer's philosophy lay a long time in the future.

He went on. The hill seemed strangely unreal, after all that he had seen from it, the whole enormous tomorrow of the cosmos. He would never quite fit into the little round of days that lay ahead.

Taury—her bright lovely face floated before him, he thought he heard her voice whisper in the cool wet wind that stroked his hair like her strong, gentle hands.

"Good-bye," he whispered into the reaching immensity of time. "Good-bye, my dearest."

He went slowly up the steps and in the front door. There would be Sam to mourn. And then there would be the carefully censored thesis to write, and a life spent in satisfying work with a girl who was sweet and kind and beautiful even if she wasn't Taury. It was enough for a mortal man.

He walked into the living room and smiled at Eve and MacPherson. "Hello," he said. "I guess I must be a little early."

Ballade of
an Artificial Satellite

THENCE THEY SAILED FAR TO THE SOUTHWARD ALONG
the land, and came to a ness; the land lay
upon the right; there were long and sandy
strands. They rowed to land, and found there
upon the ness the keel of a ship, and called the
place Keelness, and the strands they called
Wonderstrands for it took long to sail by them.

> —Thorfinn Karlsefni's voyage to Vinland,
>   as related in the saga of Erik the Red

One inland summer I walked through rye,
a wind at my heels that smelled of rain
and harried white clouds through a whistling
   sky
where the great sun stalked and shook his
   mane

and roared so brightly across the grain
it burned and shimmered like alien sands.
Ten years old, I saw down a lane
the thunderous light on Wonderstrands.

In ages before the world ran dry,
what might the mapless not contain?
Atlantis gleamed like a dream to die,
Avalon lay under faerie reign,
Cíbola guarded a golden plain,
Tir-nan-Og was fair-locked Fand's,
sober men saw from a gull's-road wain
the thunderous light on Wonderstrands.

Such clanging countries in cloudland lie;
but men grew weary and they grew sane
and they grew grown—and so did I—
and knew Tartessus was only Spain.
No galleons call at Taprobane
(Ceylon, with English); no queenly hands
wear gold from Punt; nor sees the Dane
the thunderous light on Wonderstrands.

Ahoy, Prince Andros Horizon's-bane!
They always wait, the elven lands.
An evening planet gives again
the thunderous light on Wonderstrands.